THE EAGLE HAS LANDED

WHAT IF ANIMALS TOOK OVER?

A Wildly Funny and Eye-Opening Tale of Life, Satisfaction, and the Human Struggle

BY

ALLIANCE B. ASABA

Library of Congress Reg. # 2025919206

Cover Design by: Authors Hike

Publisher: Authors Hike

For permission requests, please contact: asabaalliance@gmail.com

Dedication

"To all the dreamers who dare to question the status quo,

And to those who find humor in the absurdity of life—

This is for you..."

Acknowledgment

This book would not have been possible without the countless moments of observation, the musings of great minds before me, and the sheer ridiculousness of human nature...

A heartfelt thank you to my family and friends who entertained my wild theories, to the ginger tea that kept me awake, and to the animals who unknowingly inspire us all...

And to you, dear reader—may you find both wisdom and laughter while reading the book...

Table of Contents

Chapter 1
The Human Dilemma

The day humanity officially lost its mind was the day someone invented a $500 smart water bottle that reminded people to drink water, because, apparently, thirst was no longer a reliable indicator. More than anything, this summed up the absurdity of the modern world. People had access to the greatest knowledge in history, yet still needed apps to remind them to breathe, gadgets to count their steps, and motivational podcasts to convince them that getting out of bed was worth it.

If our ancestors were watching, they weren't invading out of fear— they were avoiding us out of embarrassment...

My father always said,

"The wisest man is the one who knows he knows nothing."

As a child, I assumed this was just one of those mysterious sayings that old men muttered to sound important.

I'd nod politely, pretend to understand, and then run off to play. But as I grew older, I began to realize that he wasn't just being philosophical—he was issuing a warning.

Despite their intelligence, humans seemed cursed with an unquenchable thirst for more. No matter how much they achieved, something was always missing, just out of reach.

More money, more success, more happiness—more, more, more...

It was as if contentment was a disease they desperately wanted to cure. If there were an Olympic event for dissatisfaction, humans would take home the gold every time and then complain about the size of the medal.

"They built cities but forgot how to live in them."

......

"They created machines to save time, yet they never have enough of it."

......

"They invented entertainment but complain of boredom."

The irony was unbearable; they had built civilizations, conquered lands, invented machines, and sent people to the moon, yet they struggled with the simplest things: peace, joy, and balance.

The pursuit of happiness had somehow transformed into a chase for exhaustion. The greatest minds of their time worked tirelessly to make their lives easier, yet no one seemed to have time to enjoy it.

The Curse of Endless Want

The human brain, a marvel of evolution, was both their greatest strength and their biggest weakness. It was an engine that never turned off, a factory of worries and dreams working overtime.

No matter how much they acquired, the craving for more never ceased...

If they earned a raise, they wanted a promotion. If they bought a house, they wanted a mansion. If they owned a car, they needed a faster one. Contentment, it seemed, was a foreign concept, something reserved for monks on mountaintops.

A wise old pigeon once said:

"Heaven's Request Line never stops ringing—angels working double shifts just to handle the wish lists. But over at the Gratitude

Desk? There's one lonely angel, sipping tea, waiting for a thank-you that never comes."

Humans were always asking…

Never appreciating…

Social media made it more worse…

Every time a human opens their phone, they are bombarded with images of people who have more: more wealth, more success, more happiness.

Even if they had just eaten a delicious meal, they suddenly felt deprived because someone else was dining on a luxury yacht. They were playing a game they could never win, running a race with no finish line.

Even in their moments of joy, they were already planning their next conquest….

A vacation wasn't just about relaxation; it was about capturing the perfect photo to prove they had a better life than their peers.

A wedding wasn't about love; it was about outshining the last extravagant ceremony they attended. They had become prisoners of their own expectations.

The worst part?

They didn't even realize it…

They blamed their dissatisfaction on external factors—their jobs, relationships, and circumstances—when the real enemy was within…

The Weight of Expectations

From childhood, humans are conditioned to believe that success is measured by milestones, such as good grades, a high-paying job, a big house, and a fancy car. They are handed a checklist for life, and if they fail to tick every box, they are seen as falling behind.

But behind...

What?

A finish line no one can even see?

The pressure is immense. Parents push their children toward careers they may not love simply because they believe financial stability is the ultimate goal. Society praises the overworked and exhausted, while those who choose a simpler, slower life are judged for lacking ambition.

"If you aren't hustling, you aren't living!" — *Is the modern-day battle cry?*

A wise parrot once observed,

"Humans run themselves ragged chasing titles and status, but for what? I have never seen an exhausted bird bragging about how many trees it visited."

Even those who achieve the so-called **"dream life"** find themselves unsatisfied.

The promotion they worked so hard for doesn't bring the joy they expected...

The expensive house feels empty...

The happiness they were promised remains elusive...

Why?

Because they never stopped to ask themselves what they truly wanted in the first place...

The Disease of Busyness

A pigeon, perched on a city streetlight, observed the humans below with mild amusement. They darted from place to place, clutching cups of coffee like lifelines, their faces glued to tiny glowing screens. If they weren't walking briskly, they were tapping frantically, their fingers moving faster than their legs.

<u>Was this a survival tactic?</u>

"Because from up here, it looked like chaos.

Somewhere along the way, humans equated busyness with importance...

<u>Were you even doing anything meaningful if you weren't constantly working, scheduling, or multitasking?</u>

A squirrel once chuckled,

"Humans work tirelessly to save time, but then they complain they have none. Meanwhile, I spend my days collecting acorns, taking naps, and running up trees for fun. Who is really winning here?"

The concept *of* **"free time"** has become almost shameful.

If someone isn't drowning in deadlines, they must not be trying hard enough. Resting is seen as laziness, despite being a biological necessity.

Even vacations come with itineraries packed to the brim; sightseeing, activities, and structured fun. Relaxation is penciled into a schedule, then rushed through like another task to complete.

This endless cycle of doing, achieving, and overworking has exhausted humans...

<u>The irony?</u>

Most animals work only to survive, and then they simply exist...

They don't complicate things. They don't create stress where there is none. They eat when they're hungry, rest when they're tired, and play when they feel like it.

A simple, balanced life—one that humans seem incapable of adopting...

The Pursuit of More

Humans have convinced themselves that happiness is just one step away.

"If I get that job, I'll be happy."

"If I make more money, I'll be happy."

"If I lose weight, I'll be happy."

But the finish line keeps moving, and they keep chasing something they'll never quite reach.

A fox, watching a human fumble with their smartphone, sighed.

"They have everything they need, yet they still search for more. Why can't they just enjoy what's in front of them?"

A wise elephant once said,

"Contentment is not the absence of desire, but the acceptance of enough."

Humans have built entire industries around them, making people feel like they are lacking. Advertisements scream, *"You need this!"*

"Your life is incomplete without it!"

Social media makes people compare their ordinary lives to someone else's highlight reel.

<u>The result?</u>

A constant feeling of being inadequate, no matter how much they have...

Meanwhile, animals remain blissfully unaware of such nonsense.

A bird is not envious of another bird's shinier feathers!

A dog does not compare its stick collection to another dog's!

They take what they need, appreciate what they have, and live in the moment—something humans have forgotten how to do...

The Art of Living Simply

Humans have filled their lives with noise—literal and figurative. Their cities hum with traffic, their minds race with worries, and their schedules overflow with obligations. In their endless pursuit of success and comfort, they have lost sight of something important: simplicity.

A panda chewing bamboo once mused,

""I do nothing all day but eat, sleep, and roll around. And I have never been stressed. Maybe humans should try that."

Living simply doesn't mean giving up ambition or success. It means recognizing when enough is enough. It means understanding that slowing down is not failure. It means realizing that life is meant to be experienced, not just managed.

A human once asked a wise old tortoise,

"What is the secret to happiness?"

The tortoise smiled.

"Walk slow; Breathe deep; Enjoy the journey."

Perhaps, after centuries of running, it is time for humanity to stop and listen...

The Watchful Eyes of Nature

And all this had not gone unnoticed. For centuries, the animals had watched in growing confusion. They had witnessed it all, from the quiet gaze of an owl in the trees to the unimpressed stare of a house cat lounging in a sunbeam.

The endless running, the constant stress, the inexplicable need to complicate even the simplest of things...

A wise old elephant in Africa once sighed as he watched two groups of humans fight over a piece of land that neither of them truly owned.

"They act as if they'll live forever."

He mumbled, shaking his massive head.

"Do they think they can take it with them when they die?"

Asked a younger elephant.

"No, but they fight as if they can."

A fox hiding behind a dumpster in England tilted his head in curiosity as a group of men in suits shouted at each other over imaginary numbers on a screen.

"They fight over things they can't even hold?"

He whispered….

"That's ridiculous. At least when I fight, it's over an actual meal."

The Awakening

As the sun rose, the animals began their mission. Owls whispered ancient wisdom in the ears of dreaming humans. Wolves howled eerie warnings outside city limits. Dolphins disrupted shipping routes, forcing humans to pause.

Birds arranged themselves in ominous symbols above crowded streets. The humans, oblivious to the meaning, dismissed these actions as oddities of nature.

But the animals knew this was only the beginning...

The bear council convened deep in the forest, each grizzly and black bear nodding solemnly.

"They have ignored every sign," one muttered.

"Perhaps we should knock over a few more trash cans and make them notice."

"We need a more coordinated approach."

An eagle declared…

"We cannot rely on humans to understand subtleties."

A dolphin, clicking excitedly, added,

"We could start by ruining their fishing operations. No fish, no sushi. That'll get their attention."

This was not just about teaching humanity a lesson. It was about preparing for the inevitable.

If humans couldn't learn from nature's subtle messages, the animals would have to take drastic action…

And so, the world shifted—slowly at first, but with the weight of something unstoppable. Something big was coming.

For the first time, the world would hear what the animals had to say…

The Illusion of Progress

Humans prided themselves on their advancements, from towering skyscrapers to powerful artificial intelligence. Yet, what had they truly gained? For every step forward, they seemed to take two steps back. They had created faster transportation, but spent hours stuck in traffic. They built endless entertainment, yet boredom still plagued them. The illusion of progress had blinded them to their own self-imposed suffering.

A horse, watching humans struggle with traffic, snorted.

"They abandoned us for machines, and now they sit for hours, going nowhere."

Technology that was meant to bring people closer only widened the emotional gap. Relationships became virtual, real conversations replaced by text messages and emojis.

The human world, despite all its brilliance, was lonelier than ever…

A wise old parrot spoke,

"They have filled the air with wires and waves, but where is the connection that truly matters?"

Animals who thrived on natural connection could not understand this paradox.

"They hold their devices more than they hold each other," a wolf noted with sadness.

"What a strange way to live."

The Breaking Point

The animal kingdom had been patient, hoping humanity would find its way back to balance. But patience had its limits. The warnings had been sent, the messages delivered, yet humans continued down their destructive path. The time for watching and waiting was over.

"If they refuse to change, we will show them change!"

The eagle declared.

"If they cannot learn, we will make them learn."

The whales began causing mysterious disappearances of shipping containers.

"The beavers gathered by the river, constructing a massive dam to divert water away from human settlements."

Even the pigeons agreed in their secret meeting,

"Stop being annoying in cities and instead deliver coordinated messages on rooftops, and pay Attention!"

<u>The world braced for what was coming next.</u>

A reckoning was on the horizon, and nothing could stop it now…

Chapter 2
The Grand Animal Meeting

A strange tension hung in the air as if the world itself were holding its breath. The forests whispered. The oceans murmured. The skies crackled with a silent energy that even the humans, in their oblivious haste, could sense but not understand. Something was brewing. Something big.

And in the heart of the animal kingdom, the call had gone out...

A meeting was needed...

A meeting unlike any other in history...

A Mysterious Call Echoes

Something was brewing. It wasn't just the usual change of seasons or the shifting of tides. This was different—primal, inevitable, and deeply unsettling.

For centuries, the animals had watched. They had seen humans claim intelligence while making choices that defied logic. They saw forests turned into concrete cages, rivers poisoned for profit, and entire species erased as if they were nothing more than scribbles on a careless notepad. And yet, the humans were still miserable.

"They have everything," a wise old turtle once mused.

"Yet they have nothing."

The frustration had reached a boiling point. It was no longer just the elephants shaking their heads at human greed or the wolves rolling their eyes at political corruption. This was bigger. This was the moment the animals had waited for—the moment when enough was enough.

The Whisper That Changed Everything

And then, the whisper began...

A single phrase, floating on the wind, slithering through the cracks of civilization and settling into the ears of every creature who had ever suffered under human dominion:

"Dogs and cats in the US have decided to let every other animal know their plans."

No one knew exactly where it started, but it didn't matter. What mattered was the message. And for the first time in history, every species, from the deepest ocean dwellers to the loftiest birds in the sky, responded to the same call.

It was time to meet...

The summons echoed through the world in ways humans could never understand. No emails, no conference calls, no smoke signals—just instinct. Birds flocked in numbers unseen, rivers swelled with creatures making their way to the great council, and even the ants, who typically had no time for nonsense, abandoned their endless labor to march toward the unknown.

The location?

A hidden valley untouched by human hands. A place where nature still ruled, where trees weren't chopped, rivers weren't dammed, and the air wasn't thick with the stench of exhaust.

The moment was historic. Never before had the world's animals gathered in one place—not for war, not for survival, but for a singular purpose:

To discuss what the hell to do about the humans…

At the center of it all, perched high on an ancient tree, was the Eagle King, sharp-eyed and unwavering. To his left, the Lion, its golden mane gleaming in the sun, flicked its tail impatiently. To his right, the Elephant Elder, wise beyond measure, stood tall, exuding both power and patience.

The murmurs of the crowd fell silent as the Eagle King spread his wings.

"We have tolerated their ways for too long."

A growl of agreement rumbled through the beasts…

A Growing List of Complaints

What followed was an outpouring of frustration so loud it could have been mistaken for an earthquake. The animals, tired of simply observing, unleashed every grievance they had bottled up over generations.

"The humans are obsessed with power," the Tiger said, his tail twitching.

"They cut down our forests, steal our land, and then wonder why they feel lost."

"They worship their own creations!" an Owl hooted indignantly.

"Machines, money, false gods of greed. And yet, they still crave more."

"They have poisoned the rivers," the Great Whale mourned, his deep voice vibrating through the valley.

"And then they wonder why their fish taste like chemicals."

"They built walls and fences," an antelope added, shaking her head.

"As if they own the land itself."

"They wage war over invisible lines on a map," a wise old tortoise muttered.

"Yet, they share the same sky, breathe the same air, and drink the same water."

"And they've done it all for what?" an Elephant Elder rumbled.

"They hoard wealth, yet they starve. They have medicine, yet they suffer. They seek peace, yet they war."

Even the tiniest creatures had their say.

"They scream when they see us," a spider muttered bitterly.

"Then they try to kill us. I'm sorry, did I trespass in your territory? Because from where I'm standing, you built your house on my web!"

"Their obsession with pesticides is infuriating," a honeybee buzzed.

"Without us, they don't eat! And yet, they keep killing us."

"They take our fur, our feathers, our skins," a crocodile hissed.

"As if we were made for their fashion."

The ***Eagle King*** let the voices rise, allowing every grievance to be heard. The anger, the confusion, the heartbreak—it had festered for too long.

And now, something had to be done…

The Grand Strategy Unfolds and The World Wakes to Confusion

The Eagle King raised a talon.

"Enough talk. If we are to do this, we must do it right. Not with violence, not with destruction. We will not become them."

A low growl of agreement spread through the crowd.

"The eagles will spread the word," the Eagle King continued.

"The wolves will reclaim the forests. The whales will control the seas. The pigeons—" He sighed.

"You will do what you do best: Be annoying. But in a strategic way."

The pigeons nodded, honored.

The world had been out of balance for too long.

And now, the reckoning had begun.

Birds disrupted morning commutes by swarming intersections, causing cars to come to a halt in a flurry of honking. Elephants positioned themselves in city streets, blocking highways and causing mass confusion.

Cats, those silent yet calculating creatures, knocked over important documents and computer servers in government offices, disrupting entire economies.

Cows stopped producing milk. Dogs, those ever-loyal companions, simply sat and stared at their owners when commanded. There was no rebellion, no violence—just refusal.

More and more animals joined the disruption. Monkeys infiltrated city centers, flipping traffic lights into chaos. Bats swarmed office buildings, setting off alarms. Whales coordinated mysterious blockades of ships, halting maritime trade.

With each passing day, humans became more unsettled. Their world was shifting, and for the first time, they weren't in control.

The Dawn of a New Order

The world of humans had become a world of animals. It was no longer just an idea—it was reality...

The old structures of society were failing. Humans were panicked, running in circles, searching for meaning in a world they no longer controlled.

"We always knew they needed us."

A sheep mumbled as a group of humans tried and failed to herd the cows back into the barn.

"Now they know it too."

But the animals weren't cruel. They had no intention of punishing humanity. Instead, they wanted to show them another way.

A better way...

The great whales spoke of the wisdom of the deep.

"You humans look outward for meaning, but true peace is found by looking within."

The lions, rulers of the wild, taught lessons in strength without greed.

"Power does not mean destruction. It means responsibility."

Even the smallest creatures had something to offer. The ants, ever industrious, demonstrated the value of cooperation over competition. The bees, crucial to life itself, reminded humanity that everything is connected.

As days passed, some humans began to listen. They observed the balance in nature, the quiet order that had existed long before them.

A New Understanding Begins

Not all humans resisted the change. Some began to see the world through a different lens. Farmers embraced more natural ways of growing crops. City dwellers left their cars behind, opting instead to walk or bike. Factories slowed production, and pollution levels began to drop.

The oceans, once murky and filled with waste, began to clear. Rivers ran fresh again. The air smelled sweeter, and the forests flourished.

For the first time in centuries, the earth was healing...

The Eagle King's Final Message

Standing on the highest branch of the ancient tree, the Eagle King addressed the world one last time. His voice was strong yet filled with wisdom and restraint.

"This was never about power," he declared.

"It was about balance. We were never meant to rule over you, only to remind you of what you had forgotten."

With that, the animals began to return to their homes. The takeover had served its purpose, and now, it was up to humanity to decide its future.

As the sun set over the valley, a quiet peace settled over the world.

Perhaps, just perhaps, the humans had finally learned their lesson.

But high above, the eagles had already taken flight, soaring across the lands, preparing for what came next.

The message had been sent—now, it was time for the world to listen.

The real challenge was only just beginning...

Chapter 3
A World United by Animals

Alright, so the Grand Animal Meeting... Man, what a scene. When it finally wrapped up, you could sense the energy lingering in the air.

It wasn't just, like, a regular meeting, you know?

It was this huge shift, this turning point, where the animals were basically saying, *"Okay, we've had enough of just watching. It's time to do something."*

There was this real mix of frustration – like, *"Seriously, humans, what's your deal?"* – but also this super strong sense of determination.

You could sense it in the little things, too. The way the wind seemed to carry their words across the valley, the way even the ocean waves had this kind of... I don't know, serious rhythm. It was like the whole world was holding its breath, waiting to see what would happen next.

And then the Eagle King climbs up to the highest branch of this ancient tree – a massive thing that looked like it had seen a million years – and he **commands** everyone's attention. He spreads his wings, and it's like the sun itself is shining just for him.

He has a booming voice, but it also contains wisdom, you know?

As if he's seen a lot and thought a lot. And he says,

"Alright, we've spoken our piece. We've laid out all the ways you humans are messing things up. Now, we've got to take that message and spread it far and wide. We've got to reach every single human

who's still willing to listen."

The Call for Messengers: Who's Gonna Tell 'Em?

That's when things got really intense. Because the big question was, who was gonna be the messengers? Who was gonna be brave enough – and, let's be honest, kinda crazy enough – to go out there and try to talk some sense into us humans?

Think about it: it's not exactly easy. We're a weird bunch. We can be brilliant, but we can also be incredibly dense. We build these amazing things, but then we trash the planet. We claim to want peace, but we're always at odds.

It's like trying to explain quantum physics to a goldfish...

So, the Eagle King stands there, and you can feel the weight of his decision. He's choosing who's gonna carry the hopes of the entire animal kingdom on their shoulders.

And then he says it: *"Eagles, you will be our messengers! Your wings will carry our words, your eyes will witness the state of the world, and your spirits will embody our unwavering commitment to change."*

A collective gasp goes through the crowd. I mean, it makes sense, right? Eagles are majestic. They're strong, they're fast, and they've got that incredible perspective from up high. They can see the big picture.

But still, it's a huge responsibility. And you can see it in the eagles who step forward. They're proud, sure, but there's also this... almost a sense of awe, you know?

"Wow, is this really real?"

Eagles of Destiny: The Chosen Ones

And it's a diverse group, too. You've got the old and the young, the experienced and the eager. It's as if they're assembling a team of all-stars.

There's **Zephyr**, this *ancient* eagle. His feathers are almost silver, and his eyes... man, his eyes have seen some stuff. He has witnessed the slow creep of human civilization, the way we continually expand, build, and consume. He remembers a time when the world was quieter, wilder.

Then you've got **Abibi**, this young eagle. She has this fire in her, a burning desire to make things right. She's seen the damage we've done – the polluted skies, the disappearing forests, the animals that have been pushed to the brink. She's ready to fight for change.

Zephyr, with a raspy voice that sounds like the wind whistling through canyons, tells Abibi, *"This isn't going to be a picnic, kid. We're likely to encounter many obstacles. Humans can be... stubborn. They're like a river that's carved its path over centuries. Trying to change its course? That's a serious challenge."*

And Abibi looks out at the horizon, as if she can already see the cities, factories, and all the obstacles ahead, and she says, *"Yeah, but there are good people out there, too."*

People who get it, who want a different way. We gotta believe in them.

Even the hardest rock gets worn down by water, right?

Persistence is key...

It's almost like a classic mentor-student thing, you know?

The old wisdom is being passed down to the new generation...

Uh Oh, Trouble in Paradise: Cracks in Unity

But even as the eagles are getting ready to leave, you can sense this tension building among the other animals.

That initial rush of excitement from the meeting?

It starts to fade, replaced by a multitude of different voices and opinions. It turns out that getting a bunch of animals to agree on anything is about as easy as herding cats.

Maybe even harder…

This badger is digging its claws into the ground, leaving deep marks, and it's grumbling,

"Why the eagles? They're good at flying, okay, I get that. But they don't know anything about living down here, in the dark, in the earth. What do they know about our *struggles? We build our homes underground; we feel the vibrations of every human footstep. They just fly above it all!"*

And then this massive blue whale, his voice booming out like a foghorn, echoes through the whole valley.

"And what about the oceans? We cover most of this planet! We've seen how humans poison our waters, how their ships mess with our songs, how their very existence threatens our survival. Shouldn't we *have a bigger say in this?"*

Even the little guys are getting in on the argument. This tiny cricket, chirping as loudly as it can, says, *"The birds get to fly away! They can escape the chaos. They see all the destruction from up high, and then they can just retreat to the sky. What about us? We're stuck here on the ground, feeling the impact of every single thing humans do!"*

It's a mess. It's like a family dinner where everyone's yelling at each other.

The Eagle King, though, doesn't lose his cool. He just listens, real serious, his eyes moving from one animal to another. He knew this was coming. He's wise enough to understand that unity isn't something you just *get*. You gotta work at it.

The King's Admonition: A Call for Harmony

Finally, he raises a talon – just one talon, but it's enough to silence the whole crowd. It's like everyone suddenly remembers who's in charge.

He steps forward, and his voice, when he speaks, is calm but powerful. It carries across the valley like a gentle breeze, but you can feel the weight of it in your chest.

"My brothers and sisters," he says, "we cannot let this discord divide us. We did not gather here to repeat the mistakes of humanity. We are not here to fight for power or dominance. We are here for something greater than ourselves: the balance of the world."

He reminds them of their shared purpose, the core message that brought them together: how everything on Earth is connected, how humans have disrupted that balance, and how the animals need to show them a better way. He draws on the wisdom they've gained from observing humanity – the emptiness of endless competition, the futility of chasing material things, the destructive consequences of ignoring the natural world.

"The eagles are our messengers," he explains, "But they are not our rulers. Every single one of you plays a vital role in this. The badger's connection to the earth, the whale's knowledge of the ocean depths, the cricket's awareness of the smallest details – all of

these are essential to our understanding of the world. We must listen to one another, respect one another, and use our differences to make us stronger, not weaker."

His words are like a balm, soothing the ruffled feathers and calming the troubled hearts. The tension in the air eases, but it doesn't disappear completely. It serves as a reminder that the struggle for unity is ongoing, one that requires constant effort and understanding.

The Ritual of Renewal: Letting Go to Grow

Then comes this intense part – the Renewal. It's an ancient ritual that the older eagles must undergo before embarking on their journey. It's a way for them to shed their old selves and get ready for the challenges ahead.

Zephyr, being one of the oldest, is the first to go. You can see the apprehension in his eyes, but also this fierce determination. He's heard the stories, whispered among the younger eagles – the breaking of the beak against this sacred stone, the plucking of their old, worn-out feathers, the agonizing waits for new ones to grow in.

It's like a symbolic death and rebirth, a way of letting go of the past to embrace the future…

He walks towards the stone, this massive thing that's been worn smooth by centuries of use, and he closes his eyes. You can almost see his memories flashing before him – the vast skies he has soared through, the changes he has witnessed, the urgency of their mission. And then, with a deep breath, he strikes his beak against the stone.

The sound cracks through the air, and you can feel the pain in your own body. It's a raw, visceral thing. Zephyr doesn't cry out, but his whole body trembles with the force of it. He endures it, though, driven by this powerful sense of purpose. He knows that this pain is a gateway to renewed strength, to a deeper understanding of the transformation the world needs.

Abibi watches him, her expression a mix of awe and concern.

<u>She gets it, you know?</u>

She understands that true change often requires sacrifice, that you have to let go of the old to make way for the new.

It's a tough lesson, but it's a crucial one…

Taking Flight: Heading into the Unknown

And then, finally, the day arrives. The eagles gather at the edge of the valley, their eyes gleaming with determination, their wings outstretched and ready to take flight. The air is electric, charged with this sense of anticipation.

The sun rises, painting the sky in incredible colors – gold, crimson, and orange – as if the heavens themselves are giving them a send-off. The Eagle King steps forward one last time, and his voice, when he speaks, is full of authority and love.

"Go now, my messengers," he commands, and his words echo across the valley, reaching into the hearts of every animal.

"Deliver our message with courage, wisdom, and unwavering resolve. Demonstrate to the world that change is not only possible but also essential. Remind them of the simple truths they have overlooked, the values they have forsaken, and the balance they have upset."

And then, with a single, powerful beat of their wings – a synchronized motion that stirs the very air around them – the eagles launch themselves into the sky. They circle above the valley, their silhouettes growing smaller and smaller against the vast expanse of the morning, carrying with them the hopes and dreams of the entire animal kingdom.

They are the vanguard of a movement, embodying a collective will to change the world...

<u>It's a breathtaking sight, but there's also a sense of foreboding, you know?</u>

Because the journey ahead is going to be brutal, they will face indifference, hostility, and their own doubts.

It's a long shot, but they're doing it anyway...

Echoes of the Human Paradox: What's Our Deal?

As they fly away from the familiar world of the valley, the eagles can't help but think about us humans.

It's a puzzle, really!

<u>How can a species be so smart and so stupid at the same time?</u>

<u>How can we create such beauty and inflict so much pain?</u>

Zephyr, his new beak gleaming in the sunlight, remembers the words of that wise old pigeon from the meeting.

"They build cities but forget how to live in them. They invent machines to save time, yet they never have enough of it."

It's as if we're constantly chasing our tails, never truly satisfied with what we have.

He wonders, with a hint of despair, if humans are even capable of hearing the animals' message.

<u>Have we become so deafened by the noise of our own world that</u>

Abibi, though, she's more optimistic. She recalls those fleeting moments of connection she's witnessed – a child's wonder at the sight of a butterfly, an old woman's tears at the sound of a whale's song, a young man's quiet contemplation of a starry night. She believes that deep down, humans still yearn for the simplicity, balance, and connection to nature that animals embody.

She holds onto a quote she once overheard from a human book: *"The cure for the world's ills lies in the quietness of the soul." She thinks maybe if they can just reach our souls, there's still hope.*

The First Encounters: A Reality Check

The eagles' first encounters with the human world are a rude awakening. They fly over these sprawling cities – these concrete jungles choked with smog, filled with the ceaseless roar of traffic, and teeming with humans rushing around with their faces glued to their phones. It's as if we're all sleepwalking through our lives, oblivious to the beauty and chaos around us.

The cities are a stark contrast to the serenity of the valley. It's a world of constant noise and movement, where everyone seems to be chasing something – money, success, the next shiny gadget. It's as if we've built an incredibly complex world, but we've forgotten how to simply be.

The eagles try to get our attention in subtle ways – soaring in synchronized patterns that disrupt the monotony of the skyline, perching on skyscrapers as silent observers, causing brief traffic jams with their unexpected appearances. They're trying to send a message, to spark curiosity, to shake us out of our routines.

But most of the time, their efforts seem to be in vain. We're so caught up in our own little worlds, so obsessed with our own problems, that we don't even notice them. We dismiss them as *"just birds,"* a momentary distraction, and then we return to our busy lives.

It's frustrating, to put it mildly; It's like shouting into a hurricane!

Abibi, after one particularly disheartening attempt to communicate, explodes. *"They're so blind!"*

She cries, her voice echoing with anger and sadness:

"They have eyes, but they do not see! They have ears, but they do not hear! They're so consumed by their own little dramas that they've lost the ability to perceive the world around them!"

Zephyr sighs, remembering the wisdom of the Elephant Elder from the meeting, the patience that guided their decisions.

"Patience, Abibi," he says, his voice a calming presence in the midst of her frustration.

"We must be patient. The human heart is a complex thing, capable of both great cruelty and great compassion. We must appeal to their better nature, to the spark of understanding that still flickers within them. Remember the saying, 'The darkest hour is just before dawn.'"

The Weight of the Task: Is It Even Possible?

As the eagles venture further into the human world, the sheer scale of their mission begins to weigh heavily on their shoulders. The world is vast, and humans are numerous and diverse, with their endless variations in culture, beliefs, and behavior. The challenge of reaching every corner of the earth and conveying their message to every single human heart seems almost insurmountable.

They witness the immensity of human civilization, with its sprawling cities that stretch as far as the eye can see, its factories that churn out products at an alarming rate, and its impact on the planet is undeniable and often devastating.

They see the incredible things humans have created – the art, the music, the technology, and the moments of breathtaking ingenuity. Still, they also see the destruction, pollution, inequality, and suffering that seem to plague their societies.

It's a world of stark contradictions, of dazzling beauty and profound despair...

Doubt begins to creep into their thoughts, like a shadow slowly obscuring the sun, casting a pall over their spirits.

<u>Is it even possible to change a species so deeply entrenched in its destructive habits?</u>

<u>Are they embarking on a fool's errand, a noble but ultimately futile attempt to alter the course of human history?</u>

<u>Is the animal kingdom's unwavering belief in humanity misplaced, a naive hope in the face of overwhelming evidence?</u>

These doubts echo the initial disagreements among the animals back in the valley, the struggle to maintain unity in the face of differing perspectives and priorities. The eagles, like the animal kingdom itself, are learning that the path to change is rarely straightforward.

It's a long and arduous journey, filled with obstacles both external and internal, a journey that demands unwavering faith, resilience, and a willingness to confront their own limitations.

Glimmers of Hope: Finding the Allies

And yet, even amidst these challenges and these moments of doubt, the eagles also encounter unexpected glimmers of hope, sparks of light in the darkness of human indifference. They discover that not all humans are blind to the plight of the natural world. Some individuals already recognize the imbalance, yearning for a more harmonious existence and actively fighting for a better future.

They meet dedicated scientists who are studying the devastating effects of pollution, driven by a profound desire to understand and reverse the damage humanity has inflicted on the planet. They encounter passionate activists who are raising their voices in defense of the voiceless creatures of the wild, tirelessly campaigning for environmental protection and animal rights.

They find remote indigenous communities who still live in accordance with nature's rhythms, their ancient wisdom offering a stark and sobering contrast to the destructive practices of modern civilization.

These humans, often marginalized or ignored by their own societies, offer the eagles invaluable insights and unwavering support. They share their knowledge, their experiences, and their hopes for a world where humans and animals can coexist in peace and mutual respect. They are the *"dreamers who dare to question the status quo,"* as mentioned in the book's dedication, the individuals who refuse to accept the current state of the world as inevitable, who believe that a better future is possible if only they'd open their eyes and their hearts.

This old woman, her face like a roadmap of wrinkles, each line telling a story of connection to the land, tells Zephyr, *"You animals are our teachers. You remind us of what we've forgotten – the simple beauty of existence, the interconnectedness of all living things. We have so much to learn from your ways, from your quiet strength, your unwavering loyalty, your acceptance of the natural order."*

And this young boy, barely a teenager, his eyes shining with a fierce passion for the planet, shares his vision with Abibi.

"We gotta work together," he says, his voice filled with the same youthful conviction that Abibi herself possesses: *"To heal this earth, to create a future where humans and animals can live in peace, where we respect each other and the world around us. It's not just about saving the animals; it's about saving ourselves."*

These encounters are like a lifeline for the eagles, a reminder that their mission isn't in vain. They realize they're not alone in this fight, that there are humans who are ready to listen, ready to change, ready to stand alongside the animal kingdom in their pursuit of a better world.

It's a fragile hope, a tiny flame flickering in the darkness, but it's enough to keep them going...

The Long Road Ahead: Trials and Tribulations

The eagles' journey, though, is still in its early stages. The vastness of the world stretches before them, an endless tapestry of landscapes, cultures, and human complexities. They know that the road ahead will be long and arduous, filled with trials that will test the very limits of their endurance, their compassion, and their unity.

They'll face the relentless indifference of a world consumed by its own pursuits, the stubborn resistance of those who cling to their destructive habits, and the crushing weight of despair when their message seems to fall on deaf ears. They'll witness the best and the worst of humanity, the heights of creativity and compassion, and the depths of cruelty and greed.

They'll also have to navigate their own internal struggles, as well as the disagreements that will inevitably arise when encountering different perspectives and challenges. They'll have to learn to balance their urgency for change with the patience and understanding that humans often require. They'll have to find strength in their diversity, drawing on each eagle's unique skills and experiences to overcome the obstacles in their path.

It's a huge undertaking, and there are moments when even the eagles themselves wonder if they're up to the task. But they keep flying, driven by something larger than themselves, by the unwavering belief that change is possible, that humanity can still find its way back to balance.

A Question for Humanity: What's It All About?

As they journey, the eagles carry within them not only the message of the animal kingdom but also a profound question, a riddle that echoes across the continents and penetrates the noise of human civilization:

<u>What does it truly mean to live a meaningful life?</u>

It's a question that the animals have been pondering for a long time, observing humanity's endless pursuit of happiness in all the wrong places. We chase wealth, power, fame, possessions, always believing that the next acquisition will finally bring us contentment. However, the animals realize that this chase is often futile, that true happiness lies not in what we have, but in how we live.

They see the beauty in simplicity, the joy in connection, the peace in harmony with nature…

They wonder if humans have forgotten these fundamental truths, if we've become so caught up in the complexities of our own creation that we've lost sight of what truly matters.

And so, the eagles' journey becomes not just a mission to deliver a message but also a quest for understanding, a search for the answer to this age-old question. They observe, they listen, they learn, hoping to find the key that will unlock humanity's potential for change.

The Journey Continues…

And so, with wings strong and hearts full of purpose, the eagles continue their flight across the world. Their experiences, their encounters, and the lessons they learn will shape the future of both the animal kingdom and humanity. They are the bridge between two worlds, the messengers of a new dawn, the hope for a future where all creatures can thrive.

But their journey is far from over. The challenges they face are only just beginning. The question of humanity's response hangs in the air, a constant source of both hope and anxiety.

<u>**Will we listen?**</u>

<u>**Will we change?**</u>

Or

<u>**Are we destined to continue down the path of self-destruction?**</u>

To witness the unfolding of their extraordinary odyssey…

To discover the answers to these crucial questions…

And …

To see whether the eagles can truly make a difference…

For that, you must continue to follow their path as they navigate the complexities of a world on the brink of change…

Chapter 4
The Eagles' Journey

The wind rushed under their wings as the eagles flew out of the safe valley. It stayed with them like a loyal friend, pushing them forward. Far below, the land looked like a patchwork quilt—fields of green and brown spreading out in every direction. Ahead, tall gray cities rose in the distance, strange and different from the world they knew.

Each eagle felt a mix of fear and excitement. Their hearts beat fast. They were on a mission—not just to fly, but to learn and watch. They were the eyes of the wild, carrying stories between animals and people. In many ways, they were explorers, heading into a world full of mystery.

As the sky grew darker with clouds, lightning flashed in the far-off sky. But the eagles didn't turn back. They flew on, strong and steady, knowing that what lay ahead could change everything for them and the world below.

The Weight of the Feathers

Zephyr flew in front, his sharp eyes full of old wisdom. The ritual of renewal had taken much from him, but it gave him something greater in return—strong purpose. He carried the memory of a world still wild and free, not yet touched by human hands. That world was gone now. Ahead of them was a land full of trouble.

Beside him flew Abibi, young and full of fire. Her new feathers shined in the sun, each flap of her wings driven by a strong wish to make things better. She had seen the damage humans had done—forests cut down, rivers filled with poison, animals with no place to go.

"It's a heavy thing," Abibi said softly over the sound of the wind. *"Carrying the hopes of so many."*

Zephyr nodded. *"Yes. But remember what the Elephant Elder told us: 'Even the tallest tree starts as a small seed.' Our journey will be long, but every small good thing we do can grow."*

Behind them, a young eagle named **Akiiki** flew with wide eyes and fast wings. Her voice was shaky but curious. *"Do you think humans will hear us? They always look so busy, like they can't see anything outside their world."*

Zephyr gave a dry laugh. *"Busy is a kind word. Many of them are lost, chasing things that don't last. But even in all that noise, there are still hearts that care. And that's where hope lives."*

A loud crack of thunder rolled in the distance. Dark clouds moved fast over the land below, where machines crawled across the earth like metal beetles. Fires burned in the trees, smoke rising like black ghosts.

Abibi's eyes narrowed. *"We don't have much time."*

Zephyr looked ahead, calm but firm. *"Then we fly faster. The storm is not the end—it's the test. And we will rise through it."*

With that, the three eagles soared higher, cutting through the wind like arrows of the sky. They were the last voice of the wild. And they would not be silent.

The Descent into the Gray

The first city rose ahead like a giant machine, cold and sharp. Its edges cut into the sky, and the closer the eagles flew, the louder the world became. The wind's soft music faded, replaced by the noise of people — the roar of engines, metal grinding on metal, and a steady hum that never stopped.

Abibi pulled back a little, uneasy. *"It's... hard to breathe here."*

Zephyr kept his wings steady, his eyes sharp. *"Don't judge too fast,"* he said.

"Look closely. There's good and bad in every place. There's light and there's dark. We must see both."

They moved through the city sky like shadows, quiet and swift. They dipped between the tall glass buildings and flew over busy streets. Sometimes they landed on ledges high above, watching the people far below — walking fast, staring down, always rushing.

Akiiki, the youngest and most curious, tried to reach them. She flew in wide loops, drawing shapes in the air — a heart, a tree, a river. Simple signs of peace, signs of balance. She hoped someone would look up and see.

But hours passed, and no one did.

"They don't even look up," Akiiki said sadly.

"They're too busy staring at those glowing rectangles in their hands. They don't even see each other."

Zephyr looked down at the crowds with a deep breath. *"Isn't it strange?"*

After a short pause, he said. *"The internet was made to bring people closer together to connect the whole world. But now it pulls people apart. You sit in the same room with someone, but you're both looking at someone else far away. You ignore the one person you could actually touch. How did it come to this? Whose trick is this?"*

Just then, a child looked up. Only for a second. A small girl, holding her mother's hand, pointed to the sky.

"Look, Mama! A bird made a heart!"

The mother glanced up but only shrugged and pulled the child along. *"Come on, we're late,"* she said.

But Zephyr saw the girl. Her eyes were full of wonder.

"There's still hope," he said softly. *"Not all are blind to the sky."*

And with that, the eagles flew deeper into the city, wings cutting through the gray, looking for more hearts that still dared to see.

The Girl Who Looked Up

But then, as the eagles soared deeper into the gray, Abibi spotted her.

Not just anyone…

A young girl with bright red hair and wide eyes that sparkled like morning light. She stood still in the middle of the sidewalk while the world rushed around her. People bumped past, hurrying with coffee cups and phones, but the girl didn't move.

She was looking straight up…

At them…

Abibi circled lower, curious. Her shadow passed over the girl, brushing across her shoes like a whisper. The girl gasped, but she didn't run. She didn't scream.

Instead, she smiled…

"A real eagle," she breathed, barely louder than the wind. Her eyes shone with wonder, as if she had found treasure in the sky.

Abibi felt something spark deep inside — something small but bright. Hope.

Maybe... just maybe...

And then, something strange happened. As if the girl's gaze had opened a door, other people began to slow down. Not all, but some.

An old man wearing a brown coat stopped and looked up. He pulled off his hat, held it to his chest, and stood still, eyes on the sky. A mother holding a toddler pointed upward, smiling with surprise. Even a man in a sharp suit, his face pale and tired, paused, loosened his tie, and stared at the birds above.

For the first time in what felt like forever, the city was quiet.

<u>Not silent—no, the machines still roared—but quieter.</u>

Zephyr landed gently on a rooftop, watching with calm eyes.

"It seems," he said, *"That even a tired soul can remember how to feel. Even in the deepest sleep, something inside them can still wake up."*

Akiiki zipped past, looping the sky with joy. *"They're watching now!"* she cried. *"They see us!"*

Zephyr gave a slight nod. *"Let's give them something worth seeing."*

So, the eagles danced across the sky. Not in wild chaos, but in rhythm — a flight filled with meaning. Loops of hope. Spirals of peace. Arcs of light against the gray.

And the people watched...

For five minutes… maybe ten… the screens stayed in pockets, the phones were forgotten.

In that small slice of time, hearts lifted...

The little girl, still rooted in place, whispered, *"Don't stop."*

And Zephyr, though she couldn't hear him, whispered back through the wind, *"We won't."*

A Symphony of Discontent

The journey took the eagles far beyond the city. They flew over deserts, oceans, mountains, and plains. They passed through rich green fields and dry wastelands, shining cities and broken towns.

They saw the best and worst of what people had built...

Far below, giant machines moved across farmlands like insects, cutting and collecting crops fast and without care. The land looked empty when they were done, like all the life had been pulled out of it.

They followed rivers once full of fish and song, now clogged with trash and chemicals. The water was dark, barely moving, with no sound but the quiet choking of nature.

They flew over forests blackened by fire. Smoke still hung in the air, thick and heavy. The old trees were gone. Only ashes and silence remained.

But not everything was lost...

They found people still fighting for the Earth. Scientists who spent their lives learning how every piece of nature fits together.

<u>Activists who locked their arms around trees to stop the saws.</u>
<u>And native communities:</u> *quiet, steady, wise living with the land, not against it.*

In these people, the eagles saw light...

But that light was small, like stars in a sky full of noise…

Even as they flew, they heard it, everywhere, the constant voice of discontent. A low sound, but always there…

A businessman shouted into his phone as the sun turned gold on the horizon. *"I need more money! It's not enough!"*

He didn't even glance at the sky…

A young woman stared into her screen, her voice barely a whisper. *"If only I looked better. If only people liked me more."* She kept scrolling, chasing images that weren't real.

A man sat alone outside a coffee shop, head in his hands. *"My job doesn't matter. Nothing feels real anymore. I don't even know why I'm here."*

The eagles listened from above, wings quiet. These weren't just complaints. They were songs of sadness, sung in silence.

Akiiki flew close to Zephyr, her voice full of wonder and worry. *"Why do they do this to themselves? They have so much… but it's like they don't see it."*

Zephyr looked out over the city lights below, glowing like stars with no warmth.

"It's strange," he said softly. *"They've forgotten how to be still. They chase something they already have — joy, peace, purpose — but they look in the wrong places."*

Abibi added, *"They run so fast, they don't stop to feel the wind, or taste the rain, or hear the trees talk. They traded quiet moments for noise."*

Just then, a soft sound rose through the night air — laughter. A child, barefoot in a garden, ran under a sprinkler, spinning with joy.

The eagles slowed…

There it was…

Real happiness…

Not bought. Not filtered. Just water, grass, and giggles under the moonlight…

Zephyr smiled, *"See that? That's what they've forgotten — but not lost. It's still there. Just hiding beneath the noise."*

And with that, they kept flying, wings steady, hearts open, still searching for those sparks in the dark.

A Moment of Connection

One evening, as the eagles soared above a quiet village nestled in a green valley in Africa, they witnessed a scene that pierced through the noise of human dissatisfaction.

A group of people had gathered in a circle, their faces illuminated by the warm glow of a bonfire. They weren't talking about money or success or the things they lacked. They were sharing stories, laughing together, singing songs that spoke of love and loss and the simple beauty of life.

An old woman with kind eyes played a melody on a worn-out guitar, her voice raspy but full of emotion…

A young couple danced hand-in-hand, their movements mirroring the rhythm of the flames…

A child gazed up at the stars, his face filled with wonder…

The eagles circled above, their hearts filled with a sense of peace they hadn't felt since leaving the valley. In that small circle of light, they saw a glimpse of what humanity could be, a reminder that amidst the chaos and discontent, there was still a yearning for connection, for simplicity, for joy.

Abibi, her voice soft with emotion, whispered, *"This... this is what were fighting for, isn't it?"*

Zephyr nodded. *"It is, little one...It is..."*

The Riddle of Humanity

As their journey continued, the eagles grappled with the riddle of humanity, the paradox of their brilliance, and their self-destruction.

"They create such magnificent things," Akiiki wondered as they flew above a towering bridge that spanned a vast river. *"Yet, they also create weapons that can destroy the world."*

Zephyr sighed. *"Their ingenuity is both their greatest strength and their greatest weakness. They have the potential for immense good, but they are also capable of terrible destruction."*

They soar above sprawling cities where lights blaze like a million fallen stars, and they glide over quiet villages where the rhythm of life still beats in harmony with the rising and setting of the sun.

They witness the resilience of the human spirit and the depths of its despair, the capacity for both great love and terrible hatred.

And through it all, they carry the weight of their mission...

The hope of the animal kingdom, and the burning question that lingers in their hearts...

<u>**Can humanity change before it's too late?**</u>

A City of Echoes

Their journey leads them to a sprawling metropolis, a city that pulses with a frenetic energy. Skyscrapers pierce the clouds, their glass and steel surfaces reflecting a distorted image of the sky. The air hums with the ceaseless drone of traffic, a mechanical heartbeat that never seems to slow.

Here, humans rush through the streets, their faces buried in glowing rectangles, their ears plugged with tiny buds that shut out the world. They move with a singular purpose, each seemingly disconnected from the vibrant life teeming around them.

Abibi watches them with a growing sense of unease. *"They're like ghosts,"* she whispers to Zephyr. *"They walk among the living, but they don't truly see."*

Zephyr nods, his gaze sweeping across the sea of faces. *"They are caught in a web of their own making. They chase illusions of connection while ignoring the real bonds that surround them."*

The eagles attempt to deliver their message, weaving patterns in the sky, perching on rooftops, their calls ringing through the canyons of buildings. But their efforts are met with indifference.

A businessman, barking into his phone, barely glances up as Abibi soars past...

A young couple, engrossed in taking selfies, fail to notice Zephyr's majestic silhouette against the setting sun...

Their words, their warnings, their pleas for change seem to vanish into the city's relentless noise...

Akiiki, her spirit dampened by the city's apathy, cries out in frustration. *"It's hopeless! They don't care! They're too busy, too distracted, too self-absorbed!"*

Zephyr, however, remains calm. *"Do not despair, little one. Even in the deepest darkness, there are flickers of light. We must seek them out."*

The Whispers of the Old Library

A quiet voice floated on the wind. It wasn't loud, but it tugged at something deep inside the eagles. It felt like an old memory, soft and strong, calling them toward something important.

They followed the sound, flying past busy streets and glowing lights, until they reached a quiet corner of the city. Hidden between tall buildings and covered in ivy stood an old library. The stone walls were cracked but strong. The windows reached high, shaped like the ones you'd see in an old church.

Inside, the world felt different...

It was still...

No horns... No flashing screens... No shouting... Just quiet...

 The kind that fills you up instead of pressing down. Dust floated through the warm air like tiny stars, glowing in the sunlight that came through the tall windows.

Books covered the walls. Stacked high. Some thick, some thin. Bound in leather or wrapped in soft cloth. The air smelled like old pages, wood, and something warm and safe, like memory itself.

In the center of the room, a group of people sat in a circle. No one was rushing. No one was staring at a screen. They were reading, writing, and talking to each other in soft voices. You could see it in their eyes. They were thinking. They were present.

An older woman stepped forward. Her hair was silver, and her eyes were kind yet sharp, as if she saw the truth in everything. She looked up at the eagles and smiled.

"Welcome, messengers," she said with a calm voice. *"We've been waiting for you."*

Abibi tilted her head. *"You can understand us?"*

The woman smiled again, warm and knowing, *"Not your language. But your hearts, yes. We can feel what you feel. The world is hurting. We know it too."*

Her name was **Jan**. She was the librarian. She explained that the library was a safe place. A quiet home for people who still believed in truth, in learning, in the power of words and stories.

"We're here to protect knowledge," she said. *"Not just facts, but ideas and dreams. Warnings and hopes from the people who came before us. The answers we need have been written down. We just forgot to look for them."*

The eagles stayed for a while…

They shared what they had seen from the sky…

The forests are lost…

The rivers are fading…

The people chasing something they couldn't even name…

The group listened carefully…

And then, they spoke too…

A young man, **Seth**, leaned forward. His voice was soft, but his words were strong. *"We can't just go through life and leave things* *worse than we found them. We're not here to just take. We're here to give back. That's how we make it better. That's how we begin again."*

Zephyr felt something *rise inside him…*

A lightness…

A spark…

The same feeling, he had when the Elder Elephant once told him, *"Inside every human is the power to fix what's broken."*

That power was here…

It wasn't loud…

It wasn't flashy…

But it was real…

That night, as the sky turned dark and stars appeared, Jan opened an old book and read it out loud. Her voice filled the room like a soft blanket, wrapping everyone in thought.

She read, *"A long time ago, People sat under trees. They looked at the stars. They shared stories face to face, not through wires and screens. They passed down wisdom with words, with touch, with love. We lost that for a while. But we can find it again."*

Akiiki, perched on a wooden beam above, whispered to the others, *"I wish more people knew places like this still existed."*

Jan looked up, her eyes shining. *"They do,"* she said. *"Hidden, yes. But still here. Waiting for hearts brave enough to come find them."*

The eagles flew off into the cool night, their wings gliding through the moonlight. They carried something different with them now.

Not just sadness…

Not just warning…

But a quiet kind of hope…

The world wasn't gone…

Not if people like this still remembered how to listen…

Not if they kept the stories alive…

The Song of the River

Leaving the library, the eagles follow the course of a river that winds its way through the city. Once a source of life and beauty, it is now choked with pollution, its waters sluggish and dark.

They see the scars of human industry along its banks – factories spewing smoke into the sky, concrete barriers confining its flow, and discarded waste littering its edges. The river, once a vibrant artery of the city, now seems to weep with sorrow.

As they fly over a particularly desolate stretch, they hear a faint melody, a haunting song that rises above the din of the city. It is a song of lament, a cry for help from the river itself.

Following the sound, they discover a young woman sitting on the riverbank, her fingers dancing across the strings of a worn-out guitar. Her voice, though filled with sadness, carries a powerful message of resilience and hope.

"Oh, river of sorrow, river of pain," she sings, her melody weaving around the sounds of the city. *"Your waters run weary, your spirit in chains. But I hear your whispers, I feel your despair, and I vow to bring back the beauty you bear."*

Abibi is drawn to the woman's song, her heart resonating with its emotion. She lands beside her, her presence startling the woman for a moment.

"You can hear it too?" the woman asks, her eyes widening with surprise.

Abibi nods. *"The river's pain... It's deep."*

The woman introduces herself as **Mimilo**, a musician who uses her art to raise awareness about the river's plight. She believes that music has the power to touch hearts and inspire change.

"The river has a story to tell," she explains. *"A story of loss, but also hope. I want to be its voice, to remind people of its importance, to ignite a passion for its restoration."*

Mimilo shares her music with the eagles, her songs filled with rich imagery of the river's past glory and her dreams for its future.

She sings of the creatures that once thrived in its waters, the trees that lined its banks, and the people who revered its life-giving force.

As they listen, the eagles feel a renewed sense of purpose. They realize that their mission is not just about delivering a message but also about amplifying the voices of those who are already fighting for change, those who see the beauty and potential that still exists within the human world.

The Dance of Defiance

Their journey takes them to a different part of the city, a district known for its vibrant arts scene and its spirit of rebellion. Here, they encounter a group of young dancers, their movements sharp and powerful, their expressions filled with fierce determination.

They are rehearsing in a makeshift space, their bodies swaying and leaping to the rhythm of drums and electronic music. Their dance is a protest, a defiance against the conformity and apathy that they see in the world around them.

A young man with brightly colored hair and a piercing gaze leads the group. He introduces himself as **Gege** and explains that their dance is a form of activism, a way to express their anger, their frustration, and their hope for a better future.

"We use our bodies as weapons," he says, his voice ringing with passion. *"We challenge the status quo, we question the norms, we demand change."*

The eagles watch in awe as the dancers move with incredible energy and precision...

Their movements tell stories of environmental destruction, social injustice, and the struggle for individual expression...

Abibi feels a surge of excitement. *"They're like us,"* she exclaims. *"They're messengers in their own way!"*

Zephyr nods. *"Indeed. They use their art to awaken hearts and minds, to inspire action."*

Gege invites the eagles to join them, to become part of their dance of defiance. The eagles, hesitant at first, feel the rhythm of the music coursing through their veins, the energy of the dancers kindling their spirits.

They soar and swoop around the dancers, their movements mirroring the dancers' passion and intensity.

It is a powerful moment of connection...

A merging of different forms of expression in a shared pursuit of change...

A Moment of Reflection

As the day draws to a close, the eagles gather on the rooftop of a tall building, overlooking the sprawling city. The lights twinkle below, a mixture of artificial and natural, mirroring the contradictions they have witnessed in the human world.

They reflect on their experiences, the encounters with those who are indifferent, those who are struggling, and those who are fighting for change. They grapple with the complexity of humanity, the capacity for both destruction and creation, for both apathy and compassion.

"It's a lot to take in," Akiiki says, her voice filled with a mix of exhaustion and wonder. *"Humans are... confusing."*

Zephyr sighs. *"They are a paradox, little one. But within that paradox lies hope. We have seen the darkness, but we have also seen the light. We have witnessed the indifference, but we have also encountered the passion. The journey is far from over, but we must not lose faith."*

Abibi looks out at the city, her eyes filled with a newfound determination. *"We will continue to fly,"* she declares.

"We will continue to listen, to learn, to share our message. We will be the bridge between the animal kingdom and humanity, until the balance is restored."

And as the stars begin to emerge in the night sky...

The eagles feel a renewed sense of purpose...

A quiet strength that comes from knowing...

They are part of something larger than themselves...

But then...

A chilling wind sweeps through the city, carrying with it a strange and unsettling energy. The eagles feel a tremor in the air, a sense of impending danger that sends a shiver down their spines.

From the depths of the city, a dark shadow rises, its form indistinct but menacing. It seems to feed on the city's negativity, its despair, its apathy.

The eagles exchanged worried glances…

What is this new threat?

What does it mean for their mission?

And as the shadow grows larger, casting a pall over the city…

The eagles know that their journey has taken a dangerous turn…

And…

The challenges ahead will be greater than they could have ever imagined…

The ending is yet to be written!

The symphony of life continues, and we are all invited to play our part…

Chapter 5
Perspectives from Different Continents

*So, about that **'spooky shadow'** thing that popped up at the end of the last part? That was quite **unsettling**!*

It felt like discovering a giant, grumpy dust bunny hiding under the world's couch, gobbling up all the negativity – the worries and stress, all that "Ugh, Monday again" stuff. For a moment, the eagles – Zephyr, Abibi, and Akiiki – were completely frozen. Their wings felt so heavy, as if taking a hundred-year nap might be the best way to cope with it all.

Zephyr, who's like Gandalf of our crew, wise and having experienced so much, was the first to shake it off. You could almost hear his brain working overtime, pushing past the urge to fly south and forget the whole thing.

"Okay," he told the others, his voice firm, cutting through the strange, chilly vibe that the shadow emitted.

*"**New plan**. Actually, let's speed up the old plan. This gloom isn't just one city's problem; it's sucking up bad vibes from **everywhere**."*

He recalled the Eagle King's original order – to spread the word to every corner of the world. *"We need the big picture. Like, right now. What's the word, continent by continent?"*

Abibi, the group's action hero who's always ready to jump into the fray, nodded quickly as her energy surged back. Freaking out wasn't her style; she preferred to get mad about things and then roll up her sleeves to fix them!

"Absolutely! It's time to connect with the GAG line – the Great

Animal Grapevine. I can't wait to discover what the world thinks about this human show!"

Akiiki, though still looking a bit startled, was starting to find her groove again. She chirped, *"So, basically, we're gonna do some global gossip?"* (Akiiki is the adorable, slightly naive one, always aiming to brighten the atmosphere.)

"Basically," Zephyr confirmed, with a little eagle grin. *"But, you know, for a really important reason. Team, fire up the network. Let's hear the reports."*

And just like that, the mission took a delightful turn! Forget about those subtle messages for a moment; it was time for some classic, animal-style information gathering. They tapped into everything – from the lively chatter of migrating swallows to the deep, rumbling updates from whales, and even a few *"accidentally"* dropped messages from pigeons that looked like they were a bit lost in a paper bag.

As the first reports began to roll in, the eagles nestled in for a long night. The fate of the animal kingdom, and maybe even humanity, hung in the balance, creating a real nail-biter of a situation.

A Journey to Africa - *Toothpicks, Tantrums, and Glowing Bricks*

The first reports, passed along by a delightful chain of super-efficient hornbills, came from the vibrant African savanna. An old elephant matriarch named **Tembi**, famously known for her long memory and even longer sighs (think of her as the wise, slightly exasperated grandma of the savanna), had noticed some truly peculiar human behavior.

*"You are **NOT** going to believe this,"* the message rumbled, full of elephant-style frustration.

*"Saw them cutting down a whole bunch of ancient baobab trees. Huge things, older than anything. And for what? **Fancy Toothpicks!** Toothpicks! Can you believe it? The total... waste! And the noise! Banging, crashing... gave me a headache for a week. Then they packed up their fancy machines and left a giant mess. My grand calf, **Tembo**, wondered why they need wood to clean their teeth when they have fingers. Honestly, I didn't know the answer. This 'Gloom' thing you mentioned? It's likely just tiredness from making really poor choices."*

Nearby, a sleek leopard named **Chui**, lounging on a branch with the effortless cool of a movie star, added his two cents via a monkey messenger service. *"Humans? They can be quite entertaining, though in a tragic sense. I witnessed two groups arguing yesterday. They were yelling, waving sticks, and throwing rocks, appearing very serious. I assumed it involved a tasty gazelle or the waterhole's control, right? Wrong. They were actually fighting over who could draw an imaginary line in the dirt first. It didn't even concern food! Honestly, sometimes it feels like their brains serve only as decoration. It's no surprise they're so miserable; they invent reasons to be so."*

A little meerkat lookout named **Pip** excitedly shared his report through a flurry of frantic squeaks, which were patiently translated by his friend, a wise ground squirrel named **Hazel**. Together, they chimed in at lightning speed:

"So busy, busy, busy! Always digging, building, and moving shiny rocks! They never take a break! One even tripped over his own feet while staring at a glowing brick and landed right in a puddle of warthog muck! It was funny but also sad! What's the rush? No one is after them! It's odd, very odd! I also hear a lot of deep sighs!

Quite gloomy!"

The eagles shared worried glances with each other. The African reports described humans caught up in trivial pursuits, harming their surroundings, and always hurrying about without a clear direction.

<u>Could this be a pattern seen around the world?</u>

This was starting to feel like a very strange nature documentary...

Life of Asia - *Too Busy to Breathe*

From Asia, the reports, delivered by a surprisingly organized network of city crows and mountain magpies, focused on a different kind of human weirdness: the high-pressure, super-stressed-out life.

A group of long-tailed macaques living near a temple, famous for their snack-stealing skills and sharp comments, offered this gem:

*"Dude, these humans are wound tighter than a cheap watch! I saw one, we call him '**Screamy Steve**', screaming – like, full-on yelling – at a vending machine because it wouldn't give him his fizzy drink fast enough. Then he gave it a good kick! The machine, not the drink, of course. It didn't help at all, though. He just stomped off, looking like he was ready to burst. A little while later, I saw him trying out some 'mindful breathing' from an app on his phone. Isn't that funny? They create all this stress, and then turn around and download an app to fix the mess! It's like a whole system of needless panic! The Gloom probably finds it all quite cozy here, like it's a spa day."*

From a quieter perspective, there was a wise old orangutan named **Kenji**, well-loved for his thoughtful expressions and his remarkable skill in peeling a banana with such dignity *(picture him as a furry, Zen master!).* He shared his thoughts through the gentle rustling of leaves, which were beautifully interpreted by a listening jungle fowl (a domestic cock) named **Leilani**:

"They build cages for themselves," the thought drifted through the trees. "Cages of time, cages of expectation, cages of needing **'more.'** *They climb and climb, but they never seem to reach the good stuff at the top. Maybe because the good stuff isn't* **'up'** *there, it's* **'here.'** *In the quiet moments. In feeling the sun, in sharing a meal. This shadow feeds on* **'later.'** *It can't live in* **'now.'** *"*

And, of course, the message from the Giant Panda community came through, shared with a touch of Zen-like simplicity by an adorably baffled red panda named **Mei**:

"Master Po says the humans seem... itchy. Always scratching problems that aren't there. He watches their frantic energy and wonders if they know naps exist. His advice about the **'Gloom'** *is: 'Is it bamboo? No? Then why worry? Eat the bamboo in front of you. Then nap. Problem solved.' He was very sure about this. We asked for more information, but he was already snoring."*

Zephyr let out a quiet sigh and rubbed his temples, trying to ease the tension building in his head. The reports coming out of Asia made one thing painfully clear—people were creating their own stress and ignoring the simple joys around them. It was as if they were allergic to peace, always racing toward some distant goal instead of slowing down to enjoy the moment right in front of them.

A Whirlwind Tour of Europe - *Honey Pots & Hidden Secrets*

European reports, passed around like gossip by sharp-eyed ravens and chatty sparrows, pointed to a lot of confusion and shady behavior. One clever fox named **Reynard**, who made a habit of walking past government buildings at night (he's kind of like a clever detective), shared this update:

*"Okay, listen to this. I saw some important-looking humans walk into a fancy building. They had serious faces and were saying big words like 'fiscal responsibility,' 'public trust,' and 'sustainable future.' It all sounded impressive. But later on, I saw those same people sneaking out the back door, slipping envelopes into their coats and getting into cars bigger than my den. It didn't look right. It smelled like... let's just say **'borrowed honey.'** Total hypocrisy. Around here, it's almost like the **'Olympics.'** I bet the Gloom loves that smell – that little hint of nonsense in the air."*

From the dense forests came **Fenrir**, the leader of a wolf pack whose ancestors had witnessed the rise and fall of human empires (imagine him as a stern, traditional leader). He conveyed his thoughts through coded howls, interpreted by a bilingual owl named **Athena**:

*"Their pack behavior is confusing. They build invisible fences called 'borders' and get really upset if someone crosses them without a special leaf – a **'passport,'** I think? I saw a group of them arguing for days about the shape of their shared food bowl – the **'economy.'** Meanwhile, a storm was coming, threatening them all. They were so busy fighting over the bowl design that they forgot to make their den stronger. Weird priorities. This shadow probably slides right through the cracks they make themselves."*

A delightful squirrel named **Nutsy**, famous for his incredible nut-hiding skills and a constant state of alertness *(think of him as a twitchy accountant)*, excitedly chattered to a friendly woodpecker named **Woody** as he passed by:

*"Humans hide their nuts, too! But in bizarre places! I saw one talking into his glowing brick about **'offshore accounts'** and **'tax**

havens.' Why not just bury them under a tree like normal creatures? *Much safer! And they get **SO** angry about nuts! Always counting them, worrying someone else has more nuts, trying to get even more nuts! It's exhausting just watching them! No wonder they look so gray and miserable – all that nut-stress!"*

Abibi shook her head, a growl rumbling in her chest. The European reports revealed a disturbing trend of dishonesty, greed, and obsession with wealth and power. Human often find themselves navigating through their own challenges, and you can really feel the weight of that in the reports.

Trip to Australia - *Beyond Beaches, It's Work Time*

When they finally arrived *(it seems coordinating animal communication was less urgent than an afternoon nap!),* the reports from Australia came in with a wonderfully relaxed vibe. They were delivered by a charming flock of sulphur-crested cockatoos, who appeared to find the entire situation quite amusing.

A cool red kangaroo named Skip was hanging out casually against a termite mound, looking like the ultimate chill dude, and he offered this observation:

*"Humans? I see them speeding by in their metal boxes. **Honk honk, rush rush**. I can't figure out why they're in such a hurry. Maybe the flies are really bothersome over there? It seems like a lot of hassle, though. As for me, I hop around a bit, munch on some grass, and watch the sunset. **'Job done.'** This whole slump feels draining. I just want to relax under a shady tree for a while. They should slow down, maybe enjoy a little break. Everything's going to be ok."*

A koala named **Willow**, perched high in a eucalyptus tree *(picture her as drowsy and sage-like, in a **'stoned koala'** manner),* shared this insight, thoughtfully understood from her drowsy sounds by a patient magpie *(an Australian crow)* named **Maggie**:

*"Shadows? Absolutely, there are plenty of those around! They're nice and cool, perfect for a '**cozy nap.**' Humans appear a little... fuzzy to me, like they might not have enough leaves. Or perhaps they've had a bit too many? It's a bit tricky to figure out! The key is to find a comfy branch, enjoy a tasty snack, take a lovely nap, and then repeat! It's '**pretty simple,**' right?"*

Even a platypus (egg-laying mammal native to eastern Australia) named **Down Under Dan**, briefly popping his head out of the water from his underwater foraging, gave a confused shrug, shown by frantic tail-wags to a nearby water dragon named **Lizzy**:

"Look, mates, honestly? I often find myself puzzled by what those land-dwellers are talking about. They seem to get excited over shiny things, loud noises, and strange smells. But for me, it's the soft mud, curious bugs, and the gentle bubbles of the stream—that's my slice of paradise! As for the soggy mood? No thanks! I'd happily choose swimming!"

Akiiki had to laugh at how the Australians saw things. Their laid-back attitude was a sharp contrast to the stress and chaos happening elsewhere in the world. It was like they weren't even touched by the heavy cloud of fear and worry everyone else felt. Maybe they just lived differently, and perhaps that wasn't such a bad idea.

America's Story - The Joy of Dogs and The Indifference of Cats (An Intimate Look)

Amidst all the activity, the eagles paused their efforts on the GAG line to observe things in the American way. It was clear that the dogs and cats had discovered something that the humans had somehow overlooked!

Zephyr found himself perched above a park, watching a scruffy terrier named **Buster** lose his mind over a beat-up tennis ball. His whole world was *THE BALL.* The chase, the catch, the triumphant return, the excited wiggles begging for another throw. Below, people scrolled through their phones and sighed under faint clouds of worry that only they could see. Buster? Totally oblivious. His unfiltered joy created a bubble that cut right through all the gray. Zephyr let out a sound that might have been an eagle's chuckle. Presence—that was their true *SUPERPOWER.*

Abibi, meanwhile, watched a sleek black cat named **Luna** lounging on the windowsill. Inside the house, her people were having a quiet but tense talk about money. Papers were scattered across the table, and their voices were tight. Luna let out a slow yawn, stretched with grace, and began to lick her left paw like nothing was wrong. She seemed completely above it all, calm and unbothered by the heavy mood in the room. That's when it hit Abibi—*THE PRIORITIES. Knowing what truly matters to you!*

Akiiki watched **Coco**, the fluffy poodle, flop onto her back and beg for belly rubs from **Emily**, who was buried under a mountain of homework and teen worries. Emily's hand moved half-heartedly at first, then a small smile appeared. That simple touch seemed to lift the fog around them, if only for a moment. *CONNECTION,* Akiiki thought—*so easy, no strings attached!*

A Short Recap: As the animals watch the world's troubles unfold, a few humans stand out. **Jan** brings color to life with her art, **Seth** lifts spirits with his music, **Mimilo** moves hearts through dance, and **Gege** brings people together through community work. Their creativity and kindness push back the shadows creeping over everything. The eagles see this brave stand and know that not all humans have surrendered to the darkness.

That tiny spark of hope will drive the animals to decide whether humanity is still worth saving...

The Punchline... Humanity!

The eagles gathered once more on a tall antenna, the city lights below flickering like a restless, sparkling blanket. The news from around the world, along with what they had seen with their own eyes, told a story that was both sad and strangely amusing. *It was like sitting through a long, bizarre comedy that somehow never ends!*

"So," Akiiki began, trying to sum it all up, "Tembi in Africa says they're wasteful and fight over nothing. Screamy Steve in Asia says they're stressed-out wrecks who need to chill out and take a nap. Reynard in Europe says they're sneaky liars obsessed with money. Skip in Australia says they need just to relax. And here in America, Buster is happy, and Luna doesn't care."

"Sounds about right," Abibi sighed, fluffing her feathers.

"It's the same story everywhere, just with different details. They're chasing their tails, creating their own despair, and then wondering why they feel dizzy and down."

"And the sadness just eats it up," Zephyr added with a hint of gravity.

"All that wasted energy, all that pointless desire, all that forgotten joy. It's a giant feast for that thing."

He glanced around at the others, his expression serious yet filled with determination:

"Our human friends are bravely fighting back with connection, memory, beauty, and community. That's so important. That's where the real battle lies."

He stopped for a moment, staring at the heavy shadow below that seemed to breathe with quiet pride, *"But this thing, it's so big, and it's everywhere. It's like trying to scoop out the sea with a spoon."*

He stood tall, recalling the Eagle King's command and the burden of the animal kingdom's aspirations returning to him. The responsibility of the whole animal kingdom.

"I believe," he declared, his tone brimming with timeless authority, "we need to stop just reporting this issue and take it to the highest level. Let's proceed with the next steps! It's essential that we tackle the root cause of this situation. Let's connect with ***The Great I Am*** *(It's a surprise; you will find out in the next part, so buckle up your seatbelts)."*

The other eagles nodded, their eyes filled with determination...

The laughter faded, replaced by a quiet strength...

They had everything they needed, and now the next move was clear...

It was time to go beyond what anyone thought was possible...

This choice was fraught with risks and uncertainties, and it would stretch them beyond their wildest expectations...

They thought they understood the world, themselves, but soon, they'd see how little they really knew...

The adventure was just getting started...

Chapter 6
The Petition to the Great I Am

Things started to feel a little different. High above a busy human city, three eagles are floating elegantly atop the sparkling spire of the Peak Tower. Below them, the cityscape pulsed with vibrant energy.

Yellow taxis zipped through the avenues like busy little beetles, their horns creating a cacophony of sound. Multicolored lights danced from towering billboards, showcasing everything from sweet drinks to exciting virtual experiences.

And the people...

They hurried along the bustling sidewalks, often looking down at their glowing screens, their faces reflecting a blend of concern, determination, and fatigue. The atmosphere felt alive with a tangible energy, a soft buzz of tension, worry, and the vibrant noise of city life.

However, that wasn't the most unusual part...

The Shadow's Grip: A Gloomy World

Floating through the city like a creeping, dark fog was something even stranger—*a shadow*. But this shadow wasn't a usual one, cast by a building or a cloud. No, this shadow was alive! It writhed and pulsed, with blurry edges, and seemed to be feeding on the city's energy.

Each time a human snapped at another, felt a twinge of fear, or succumbed to the weight of exhaustion, that shadow grew a little stronger, a little thicker. It absorbed the negativity like a monstrous leech, its presence a subtle, lingering concern.

Zephyr, the wise old eagle, narrowed his eyes with a thoughtful gaze. His once rich brown feathers, now charmingly speckled with white and gray, beautifully tell the story of many seasons lived. When he spoke, his low voice resonated with the weight of ages.

He turned to Abibi and Akiiki, sweeping his gaze over the chaos below.

"We need to connect with the Great I Am," he shared, his words hanging in the air like a gentle prophecy, inviting us to reflect on their depth.

Abibi, a swift and spirited eagle with eyes shimmering like molten gold, blinked in delightful surprise. Akiiki, the youngest and most excited of the trio, almost lost his balance on the antenna, his little claws softly brushing against the metal.

"Uh... say what now?"

Akiiki asked, tilting her head in a playful confusion.

"Do we, like, call a number? Is there a celestial hotline? Or do we knock on a golden door? Maybe send a text with, like, magic wings?"

Zephyr chuckled softly, his laughter like a gentle breeze rustling through ancient pines, creating a warm and inviting atmosphere.

*"No, little one. It's not like calling a helpline. There's no celestial switchboard. The **Great I Am** doesn't work that way. You don't talk with your beak, Akiiki. You talk with your heart. With your very essence."*

Abibi rubbed the feathers over her keen, perceptive eye.

"So, what—you simply... sense it? Like when we detect changes in air pressure before a storm arrives? Or how we can tell a mouse is darting around nearby, even if it's hidden in the tall grass?"

"Exactly," Zephyr nodded, his gaze intense.

"But bigger, Abibi. Much, much bigger. We're not just asking for a little help or seeking a sign. We're gearing up to make our case—a heartfelt appeal, a sincere demand—on behalf of all the animals out there."

Akiiki's eyes sparkled with wonder, mirroring the dazzling lights of the city.

"Wait, you mean like... a speech? A formal presentation? With charts and graphs? Like when those humans try to sell new snack food on TV with all those flashing images?"

"Well... kinda," Abibi said with a playful tone in her voice, *"but this one's just a tad more important than cookies, Akiiki."*

"Way more important," Zephyr agreed, grave.

"Maybe the animals could do better than humans. We have a wisdom and balance they've lost. We need everyone's help, every creature's voice, to make that case."

"Everyone? Like, the whole animal kingdom?" Akiiki flapped her wings in disbelief, almost wobbling again.

*"Even quirky **Uncle Louie** the llama? You know, the one who playfully spits when he gets a bit nervous?"*

"Yes," Abibi said with conviction.

"Even him, Akiiki. Especially him. Every single voice, no matter

how small or unique, enriches the chorus we create together."

Zephyr looked out over the sprawling city, his gaze filled with a mixture of pity and determination.

"But to do this, we need silence. True silence. Not the absence of sound, but the absence of noise. A place where we can truly hear, where our thoughts can rise, unimpeded, to the Great I Am."

And so, the three eagles soared into the sky with grace and majesty...

The Ascent to Quiet: A Call from the Heights

They beautifully departed from the bustling city—the honking horns, the screeching brakes, the dazzling flashing lights, and the relentless stress. They soared above the concrete canyons, softly leaving behind the world of steel and smoke. For days, they drifted through the sky, their magnificent wings gracefully carrying them across stunning landscapes.

They journeyed over majestic mountains with jagged, snow-capped peaks that seemed to touch the clouds like the teeth of ancient giants. They explored valleys blanketed by trees that have stood the test of time, their leaves gently whispering secrets in long-forgotten languages.

They flew over winding rivers that snaked through the earth like silver ribbons, over scorching deserts where the sun beat down with relentless fury, over icy lands where the wind howled like a hungry wolf, and over lush jungles teeming with life, a symphony of chirps, growls, and rustling leaves.

At last, after what felt like forever, they discovered it—a lofty, rugged plateau atop the world. The sky above was an endless sea of azure, reaching toward infinity. The air was thin and refreshing, infused with the fragrance of wildflowers and hints of rain. The wind hummed a tune of liberty, while the stillness was deep, interrupted only by the rare call of a soaring hawk.

"This is it," Zephyr said, his voice hushed with reverence as he landed on a wide, flat rock that appeared to have been waiting for them since the dawn of time.

The air was still, yet vibrant with a subtle energy. The world below felt distant, almost unreal. The noise and chaos of human civilization seemed like a vanishing dream.

"But how do we call all the animals?" Akiiki asked, her brow furrowed in confusion.

"We don't have phones, and there aren't any giant party invites lying around. Should we send smoke signals or maybe train a million pigeons?"

GAG Line Activated: Whispers Across the Wild

Abibi, always the practical one, flashed a warm grin.

*"Easy, Akiiki. We use the **GAG line**."*

"The what?" Akiiki asked again, tilting her head slightly in confusion as she had previously.

*"The **Great Animal Grapevine**,"* Zephyr explained, his beak curving into a gentle smile.

"It's our special way of sharing messages and connecting across great distances without needing words or wires. This beautiful network flows from our instincts and feelings, with nature giving us those gentle nudges. It's not loud or flashy at all; it's simply... known. A soft whisper in the wind, a delicate ripple in the water, a

shared understanding that vibrates in our hearts."

And so, they sent out the signals…

"Alright, friends," Zephyr whispered into the sky, his voice heavy.

"Wherever you are, stop, just for a moment. Feel the world. Think about the endless noise, the waste, the frantic rushing, the constant striving. Consider what could be better. Send that feeling up here. We need your strength and voice."

And all across the globe, something truly amazing happened…

Global Chorus: The Animal Summons

On the vast, sun-kissed African plains, **Tembi** the elephant gracefully lifted her strong trunk and let out a deep, resonant rumble. This lovely sound gently vibrated through the earth, sharing whispers of ancient wisdom and a hint of patient concern.

In the lush, steamy jungles of Asia, **Kenji** the orangutan took a moment to pause while peeling a banana. His thoughtful eyes gently closed as he gathered his reflections, sharing a wave of tranquil, arboreal wisdom into the warm, humid breeze.

In a cozy city park in Europe, nestled among manicured lawns and ornate fountains, **Reynard** the fox paused in his nightly prowl through a tipped-over trash can. His sharp nose twitched as he gave a knowing nod, a silent acknowledgment that said, *"Yep! These humans are a mess. I could run this park better in my sleep."*

In a warm and inviting American backyard, **Buster**, the golden retriever, joyfully dropped his cherished tennis ball and perked up his floppy ears. His tail thumped gently against the grass, filled with a delightful mix of unwavering loyalty and a touch of concern in his canine heart.

On a sunny window ledge in a lively metropolis, Luna the calico cat opened one sparkling emerald eye, gave a slow, deliberate blink, and conveyed her feelings with a charming air of disdainful elegance.

"Y'all are stressing me out with your constant activity. I'm going back to my nap."

From desert camels gently swaying through the shifting dunes to snowy owls cozily perched on icy branches, from bees buzzing tiredly over fields of wilting flowers to whales softly singing mournful songs to each other in the deepest, darkest trenches of the ocean—every creature, both great and small, joined in. Their thoughts, feelings, worries, hopes, and frustrations rose like a million little smoke signals. They came together in the vast expanse of the sky, heading straight for the rocky plateau where the three eagles patiently awaited their arrival.

Emotion Overload: A Tidal Wave of Feelings

The eagles experienced an overwhelming rush of feelings all at once...

It was like being embraced by a massive wave of pure emotion, a tidal surge of shared awareness...

They felt the fierce love of a *mother bear* for her *cubs*, the desperate fear of a gazelle fleeing a *lion*, the quiet patience of an *ancient tortoise*, the endless curiosity of a *playful dolphin*, and the deep, abiding connection of a *wolf* pack howling at the moon. They sensed the earth's fatigue, the silent struggles of the *forests*, the muffled cries of the *polluted rivers*, and the growing anxiety of a *world* yearning for balance.

With a deep breath, Zephyr felt his body tremble just a bit, overwhelmed by the intensity of the moment. *"Alright,"* he said, his voice now brimming with a determined spirit.

"Time to share the message… It's time to voice our thoughts for the voiceless."

They softly centered their thoughts, gently closing their eyes, and spoke—not with words that merely echoed in the air, but through a heartfelt, powerful language of spirit that beautifully resonated through the very fabric of existence.

"Great I Am," Zephyr thought, his voice a clear, unwavering beacon in the silent symphony of the universe.

"We are here, representing all living things—the creatures of the land, the sea, and the sky. Humans have been in charge, the agents of this world, for a long time. But things are… out of balance. The harmony is broken. The web of life is fraying. And we think, with all humility and respect, that maybe… just maybe… we can do better."

Abibi joined in, her thoughts flowing like a swift, sure current alongside Zephyr's.

"They take too much. They consume without replenishing. They build walls instead of bridges. They don't listen to the whispers of the wind or the wisdom of the ancient trees. They build giant boxes of metal and glass and forget what the sun feels like on their skin, what the earth smells like after the rain. We remember. We live by the rhythm of the seasons. We move with the tides. We are the heartbeat of this world. Give us a chance. Let us show them the way."

Akiiki, with his youthful energy bringing a sense of urgency to his plea, chimed in.

"We love the sky, the land, the oceans, and the forests, as well as

the deserts. We take only what we need and give back even more than we take. Our desire to help extends beyond ourselves—it's for everyone, even for the two-legged. They may have forgotten how to be part of the circle, but we remember, and we're here to teach them!"

As their thoughts soared, the air around them began to shimmer and vibrate with an incredible, unseen energy. The sky seemed to brighten even more, with blue deepening into a beautiful, almost celestial hue. The plateau itself seemed to glow warmly from within, radiating a delightful warmth that was both comforting and awe-inspiring.

And then, just like that, it happened...

The Great I Am Answers: A Sacred Offering

There wasn't a booming voice from the heavens, nor was there a grand trumpet fanfare, or even a blinding flash of lightning. Instead, what was present was something much more profound and extremely powerful.

It's just a feeling—*a deep, resonant presence that beautifully fills their minds, their hearts, and their very being.*

It's the kind of presence that invites you to sit still in wonder, listen with every fiber of your being, and hold your breath in reverence.

A message filled their minds, shimmering like crystal, yet as vast and mysterious as the universe itself:

"We are listening and truly value your thoughts!"

The eagles didn't speak...

They held onto the silence...

Allowing the words to resonate within them and sink into the deepest recesses of their souls...

Then, the Great I Am continued, and the feeling grew richer and more defined, becoming even more focused with each moment.

"Your thoughts are heard. The cries of the world, the pain of the creatures, the imbalance... it has not gone unnoticed. The human project, as you call it, is... unsteady. Precarious. At a crossroads."

"Your request to take over is... bold," the presence continued, a hint of playful amusement, or maybe a challenge, woven into the thought.

"Bold, even... you claim to understand the natural world better than those who were entrusted with its care. You believe your way is wiser, more sustainable."

Abibi nodded, her golden eyes sparkling with steadfast belief.

"Because we live it. We are it. We are the natural way. We are the embodiment of balance, of harmony, of the interconnectedness of all things."

"We see that," the presence acknowledged warmly.

"We truly appreciate your connection and the wisdom you bring. However, it's important to remember that claims need proof, not just words. And let's not forget: You've never walked in their shoes. You may not fully understand their struggles, burdens, triumphs, or failings."

Zephyr sensed a sudden chill, a coldness that seemed to come from somewhere beyond the mountain air. The wind, once so calm, now picked up speed, swirling around them with a disconcerting intensity.

A Challenge Issued: Walking in Another's Paws

"Here is the plan," the Great I Am declared, the words ringing in the eagles' minds with the power of a cosmic decree. *"The humans… will live as you do."*

The eagles let out gasps, their feathers rustling in surprise. This wasn't quite the answer they had expected.

"They will see through your eyes. Feel through your skin. Hear through your ears. For a time, their tools, their power, their money, their technology… all that they grip to so tightly… will be gone. They will find themselves stripped bare, relying on their instincts, the beauty of nature, and their own unique abilities. They will learn to live with the rhythms of the earth, with the limitations they have so long ignored, with the interconnectedness they have forgotten."

"They will walk in your feathers," the presence concluded, the words hanging in the air like a heavy weight.

A moment filled with anticipation followed, a silence that stretched to the universe's edges…

Then, with a certainty that allowed for no debate, the presence kindly stated:

"Phase one: begin."

And just like that, the presence gently faded away, leaving behind an air of mystery…

The sky gently shifted back to normal, with the intense blue softening into a lovely hue.

The air settled down, and the wind quieted as quickly as it had danced through the trees.

Yet, everything felt different…

The world had ever so slightly shifted on its axis, and the eagles sensed, with a deep and reassuring certainty in their bones, that everything had transformed.

The eagles looked at one another, their faces reflecting a blend of wonder, disbelief, and a growing sense of unease.

"Did… did we just change everything?" Akiiki asked quietly, her voice soft and almost hesitant. Her youthful bravado had given way to a deep sense of wonder mixed with a touch of fear.

Abibi's feathers puffed up, giving her normally sleek form a slightly untidy look. Her golden eyes shimmered with surprise.

"This wasn't… this wasn't exactly what we planned, was it? We just wanted to share our thoughts, to express our perspective… not… not turn the whole world upside down."

Zephyr took a moment before responding, his eyes exploring the horizon, lost in thought. His ancient mind wrestled with the enormity of what had just unfolded. Deep in reflection, he resembled a wise old sage pondering the vast mysteries of the cosmos. After a pause, he finally spoke, his voice calm and steady, infused with a gentle resolve.

"Plans can change, little ones. The world does too, and so must we! What truly matters now isn't what we anticipated, but how we choose to respond together. Let's focus on guiding this change and helping each other navigate the storm that is about to break."

They stood there for a long moment, three small figures perched on the edge of a silent precipice, while the world below teetered on the brink of something excitingly new.

The hopes and dreams of every creature gently rest upon their feathered shoulders…

The Unwritten Path: A Collision of Two Worlds Begins

Zephyr gazed up at the sky, which was beginning to dance with mysterious, unseen currents. A fresh energy buzzed in the air, creating a thrilling sense of anticipation along with just a hint of unease.

"We watch," he said, his voice steady and reassuring. "We wait. And when the time comes… we're here to help them find the way. We become their guides, their teachers, their… their conscience."

Across the globe, the transformation was well underway. Unfamiliar changes emerged like wildflowers after a storm, initially subtle but increasing in intensity with every moment. People started to stir, blink, and glance around, feeling a new sense of disorientation, with heightened senses and altered perceptions. They no longer felt entirely… *human.*

The world held its breath as the shift began—not with a loud crash, but with a soothing hum, a tide that gracefully washed over everything, changing reality. Cities twitched in excitement, forests listened curiously, and oceans stirred with ancient anticipation. Something timeless was being remembered, and something new, wonderfully wild and untamed, was about to be *born.*

The test had begun, and the challenge was evident…

A crucial question had arisen, one that would determine the destinies of two worlds:

<u>How would humans respond when the world they shaped no longer followed their rules?</u>

<u>How would they react when stripped of their power and forced to confront nature's raw, untamed reality?</u>

Animals excited for change inspire an unbelievable evolution...

As humans are on the edge of uncovering what it really means to be part of their world...

Get ready for the twist that's coming next...

Chapter 7
The Test of Humanity

When the Great I Am uttered the words, *"Phase one: begin,"* it was not just a command. It was a spark that lit the fuse of an invisible revolution. The world didn't shake with loud thunder or break beneath us. Instead, it flowed softly, like a gentle breath gliding across the Earth. Although unseen, its effects profoundly affected the skin, bones, and core of everyone alive.

All at once, humanity sensed something was very wrong or maybe very right…

The Great Flip Begins

Something ancient awakened, surging through the air as a silent shockwave reaching every soul, regardless of geography, status, or belief. This wasn't a disaster, but a spiritual correction.

From the majestic mountaintops draped in snow to the sun-drenched deserts, change arrived unexpectedly. It didn't feel like a punishment but rather a moment of revelation. As reality blended together, the curtain was drawn back, and the human world started to unravel—not through fire or flood but from the irresistible power of truth.

High above, *Zephyr, Abibi, and Akiiki* perched on their cliff, feathers tight, hearts beating. They observed as the initial wave of transformation swept through cities, towns, and rural areas alike.

It didn't look like fire or war…

It looked like *confusion*, like people waking up from a *lifelong sleep* and realizing the dream they'd been in was a *lie*.

"It's starting," Abibi whispered, her talons gripping stone.

"And they have no idea what's coming next."

"They never saw it coming," Zephyr replied.

"But now they must face themselves."

Sensory Overload: Reality Unfiltered

It started gradually, but soon it escalated in intensity!

Colors radiated vibrantly, sounds danced playfully, and scents enveloped the senses…

The world transformed into something vivid and alive…

A stockbroker in New York screamed, not from pain, but from the assault of sensation. He sensed tension in the air—*his intern's anxious sweat, the bitter aroma of his boss's coffee breath, and the scent of betrayal around the dollar bills in his briefcase.*

The buzz of the trading floor became unbearable—*each ring of a phone like a gunshot, each voice like a lion's roar.*

His voice cracked as he dropped his Bluetooth headset. *"What is that smell?"* he gasped. *"Why do I feel like I'm in a zoo?"*

Across the world, in Paris, a fashion blogger reeled from the brightness of her croissant. The vibrant colors of her breakfast table made her nauseous. Her first instinct was not to photograph but to fluff and preen—an atavistic urge to display, to survive, to be noticed. Her breath caught.

"Why do I want to spread my arms? What... what is this feeling?"

"Birds sing not because they have answers," Zephyr whispered, watching from above, *"but because they have songs. The day*

humans understand that they should smile, not because they have no challenges, but because there is hope, they may find peace."

Akiiki tilted her head and said, *"Why don't they have their own songs? All I hear is noise."*

Abibi replied, *"They've been singing someone else's tune for too long."*

The Death of Distraction

Then came the silence...

No warning... No countdown...Just stillness...

As phones went dark and screens blinked out, the internet vanished like a wisp of smoke. Cars came to a halt in the middle of the road, and planes fell from the sky like birds with broken wings. Elevators paused between floors. The heartbeat of modern life is gone, and with it, the illusion of control.

A billionaire stood frozen, clutching his dead iPhone as if it were a baby that wouldn't wake up.

His wallet, which was once thick with money, now felt as empty as crumpled leaves blowing in the breeze. He glanced around, a bit lost in thought, when suddenly he noticed a stray dog sniffing the air. Its eyes sparkled with calmness, focus, and a lively spirit.

The dog knew; the man didn't!

For the first time, he experienced a feeling of smallness, stripped of wealth and power, simply feeling helpless.

Abibi stood nearby, quietly observing the unfolding scene with a gentle but firm presence in his voice.

"They chased power through symbols... Phones... Money...

Wires... Titles... Now those symbols mean nothing."

Zephyr nodded thoughtfully, reflecting, *"The day humans learn that the power of love is stronger than the love of power—that's when peace will come."*

A Primal Awakening

In classrooms, teachers suddenly fell silent, staring at empty spaces as chalk slipped from their hands. In the halls of power, leaders froze mid-sentence, their words lost. A politician stood still, watching a moth fly in circles, caught in the soft light. In a kitchen, a top chef dropped his knife, his hands trembling as he sniffed a raw carrot, feeling a strange urge to bite into it whole.

Something big was waking up...

It rushed through people like a *wild* wave. They sniffed the *air*. They scratched their *arms*, moving like *animals*. They walked *barefoot*, felt the ground beneath their feet, crouched low, and stared at the sky, as if seeing it for the *first time*. Some cried, some growled, and others curled up under trees, letting go of words but remembering the feel of bark, the *taste of earth*.

A woman dropped her designer purse and whispered, *"Why did I ever think I needed this?"*

An old man kicked off his shoes and said, *"The ground... it feels alive."*

Zephyr watched from above and whispered, *"They're waking up. But waking isn't easy."*

Akiiki added, *"It's like the past is crawling back into them."*

The Collapse of Status

The flip didn't seem to mind who anyone was. Even the *Famous*

Personalities showed signs of fear, and *Generals* found themselves in tears. *Influencers* were still around, but their presence faded into the background as people lost interest.

Their spotlight was gone…

People didn't need idols who couldn't hunt, build, or heal…

In a quiet park, a former CEO begged a squirrel for a piece of a nut. The squirrel blinked, then ran.

The CEO dropped to his knees and cried.

Zephyr glanced down and said, *"The more you learn about the dignity of the animal kingdom, the more you want to avoid people."*

"They were taught to forget who they really are," Abibi said quietly.

"Now they've got to wake up and remember."

An actor who used to make everyone laugh in romantic comedies was now perched in a tree, whistling to birds like they were old friends…

A tech billionaire was curled up in a barn, eyes closed, listening to cows breathe like it was a bedtime story…

Zephyr glanced around, his voice steady but sharp:

"Fame was all just noise. They were trained to forget who they really are. Now? Now they've got to wake up and face the truth. No more likes. No more followers. Just who they truly are when the spotlight fades."

Chaos with Purpose

It wasn't just chaos for chaos's sake; it served as a wake-up call. All the things that humans believed were so important—*titles, rankings, social status* were gently burned away in the illuminating fire of truth.

And from the ashes, something soft and fragile began to emerge.

A girl fed a stray cat, not for likes or attention, but simply because she cared... A man planted a tree, not to make a profit, but to give something back... A mother held her child, not distracted by the world, but fully present, in the moment...

"This is the test," Zephyr said quietly.

"Not the pain, but the presence. Not to endure suffering, but to witness it. To strip away the noise and train your eyes to see clearly again. Attention is the lesson—we just forgot how to pay it."

The Wisdom of the Wild

In the animal kingdom, rules are simple: *eat when hungry, rest when tired, and protect what you love.*

"Open their eyes and ears to truth," Abibi said, *"Close them to deception and distraction, and they will save themselves from a chaotic life."*

Akiiki nodded with a curious look, *"Do you think they can do it?"*

Zephyr sighed, *"I don't know. But hope is a stubborn bird."*

In that moment, spanning a hundred rooftops, hills, and trees, animals waited...

Observing...

Praying...

Holding space...

Phase one had already commenced...

The trial of humanity was in progress…

And for the first time in generations, the future remained unwritten…

The Primal Scream Within

It wasn't only society that fell apart; it was our very identities. Humanity was brought down to its core essence, revealing what truly matters.

Once ***influential leaders*** who had ruled empires from sleek ***glass towers*** hours before now nervously sought refuge in shadowy alleys. Though their polished shoes showed some scuff marks, and their designer watches seemed to have lost their charm, they still held a certain story behind them. Some sniffed at tree trunks like puzzled hounds. Others curled beneath benches, issuing deep, guttural sounds of fear.

A **fitness expert** in ***San Francisco***, who had tracked every calorie, every step, now crawled through a park, chasing the scent of wild berries. His smartwatch blinked its final warning, then died. And in the quiet that followed, he actually heard his breath—something he hadn't noticed in years.

Thousands of miles away, a ***librarian*** in ***Prague*** stood frozen in a room full of fallen books. Knowledge meant nothing now. A raven landed on the windowsill. It stared. She stared back. Then she slowly nodded, like she finally understood something words could never say.

The chaos outside mirrored the storm inside…

There were no meetings to attend, no deadlines to meet, no roles to play…

Only the raw, primal urge to survive—and maybe, just maybe, a sudden hunger for something real, something that mattered...

Rediscovering What Was Lost

A group of **kids** in *Kenya* gathered in a circle under a tall acacia tree, humming together without even knowing why. Their laughter filled the air as their hands became covered in mud, and their faces shone brightly with joy. No phones, no distractions—*just the pure fun of their own little world.*

Meanwhile, in *Tokyo*, a **man** in a crisp business suit lay down in a shallow stream, staring up at the sky. As the clouds drifted by, he silently cried—*not out of sadness*, but because, for the first time, he felt a deep, peaceful connection to the world around him—*not above it, just part of it.*

In *Mexico*, a **grandmother** who once spent hours shopping online was now showing her grandchildren how to grind maize with stones. The flour flew, dusting their faces as they giggled together. She smiled, not for the cameras, but because something deep inside her had been awakened—*a connection to a time long passed.*

Abibi watched the moments unfold from above, eyes full of wonder.

"Some are starting to remember," he said, voice low like a breeze before rain.

Akiiki nodded, a small smile tugging at her lips.

"And some... they're waking up. Like the earth after a long sleep."

Zephyr's wings stretched wide, catching the wind.

"The day they choose the quiet song of the wind over the roar of profit—that's the day they'll truly come home to themselves."

The Judgment Without Violence

Even when everything seemed to fall apart, there were no bombs, no battles, no armies. Just a strange kind of stillness.

<u>The real fight?</u>

It was inside…

In **Istanbul**, a **man** lowered his body and remained in that position. He whispered his gratitude for simply being alive and able to breathe.

In **New York,** a street artist picked up her paintbrush once more— *not for likes, not for money, but because the colors were calling her back.*

All around the world, people began to truly look at each other, not just glance—*they looked.*

They saw fear in each other's eyes, but also hope, loneliness, and something else—*light.*

For the first time in a long time, some people reached out a *hand* instead of *scrolling past.*

Abibi's eyes glimmered, *"There is strength here, beneath the confusion."*

Akiiki nodded thoughtfully, sharing, *"They just forgot. They believed they were machines."*

"Now they must become beings again," Zephyr said, *"not human-doings, but human beings."*

It's a gentle reminder to embrace our true selves and find joy in being rather than just doing!

Waking the Soul

A preacher in Georgia stepped down from his pulpit and walked into the town square. No microphone, no sermon, just real stories told from the heart—*raw, honest, and unpolished.*

Across the world, a woman in Egypt removed the mirror from her bedroom. Tired of chasing someone else's image, she stepped outside and danced barefoot in the sand—*finally free.*

In Australia, as the sky turned a haunting shade of orange, surfers didn't run. They grabbed their boards and paddled out—*not to escape, but to feel a deeper connection.*

Above them all, birds danced gracefully in the sky, and the wind whispered gently, soft as breath…

Zephyr whispered, *"This was never about how much you knew. It was always about how much you cared. Not the facts in your head— but the truth in your heart."*

The Return to Earth

Without cars, people walked…

Without digital maps, they followed stars…

Without the internet, they turned to each other…

They revived cherished traditions by gathering around warm fires, sharing stories, and marveling together at the moonrise, present and free from screens. They shed tears—*not from sadness, but from the joy of rediscovering what truly matters.*

Zephyr turned to his companions. "This is not the end. This is the beginning."

Abibi glanced down at a child happily planting a sapling beside the ruins of a mall, *"Look at that, a seed, growing in the ashes!"*

"They are learning," Akiiki said softly, *"to live not as kings of the world, but as part of it."*

A Final Word of Hope

There was still a struggle… Still a confusion… Still a fear…

<u>But for every breakdown, something small and hopeful began to grow.</u>

A flute echoed down the streets of Rome…

In Berlin, steam rose from a shared pot of soup…

In Gaza, a mural of peace bloomed across a broken wall…

"The birds don't fly to escape the storm," Zephyr said.

"They fly because they still believe in clear skies."

He glanced up at the stars.

"And now, maybe… they do too."

The Great Flip was still happening—*still shaking things up. But now, its message had landed in the heart of humanity.*

Phase Two *was on the way…*

And this time…

Humanity had a choice to make…

Chapter 8
The Reality Check

At first, the animals were full of excitement, but when the *Great I Am* flipped things around and humans started to lose control, it felt like a victory for them all. The world had transformed in a way that filled them with pride; *the atmosphere crackled with energy.*

Abibi, Zephyr, Akiiki, and their eagle friends soared above the continents, marveling at the unfolding events. Animals from all around the Earth—forests, rivers, oceans—came together to witness the amazing events that had taken place. The cities felt quiet, like a silence wrapped around them. It was hard to believe what they experienced.

The Euphoria of Possibility

For the first time in history, no rattling chains or clicking cage doors were heard. Zoos stood silent, farms lay empty, and forests remained intact. Elephants roared in the wild, wolves howled in celebration, and birds sang with newfound confidence. It felt like the world was finally getting what it deserved.

"Look at them," Akiiki said, her golden feathers shining bright in the sunlight. *"They seem a bit lost, barefoot, and feeling confused. Meanwhile, we have the joy of soaring through the sky!"*

Abibi looked down, too, nodding slowly. *"They're humbled. And they don't even know it."*

Zephyr stayed quiet, watching the scene below him. He saw a **general**—someone who used to lead soldiers—crouching in a bush, picking berries without knowing whether they were safe.

He observed a famous *movie star* trying to catch fish with her bare hands. She was frustrated and crying. It hit him hard. The humans, who once had everything, now found themselves feeling a bit lost. Without their gadgets, machines, or even their former status, it all felt a little overwhelming.

New Bosses, New Messes

It didn't take long for some animals to start thinking they could do better than humans had!

Some of them saw an opportunity. They thought, why not try running things now?

In *Australia*, a lively group of *crows* chose to hold an exciting meeting of their own! Having observed humans in boardrooms for years, they thought they had a pretty good grasp of how those meetings worked. Now, with all the human chairs left empty, they eagerly hopped into the room.

They had fun playing with the presentation clickers, pecking at buttons, and nodding at each other as if they were the most important beings around.

But things didn't go as planned...

One *crow* shouted over the others. Another one was so excited that he kept flying around the room in circles. The PowerPoint never started; it was a total mess.

In *Nairobi*, a group of *owls* tried to hold a session in an actual parliament building. With their wisdom and seriousness, they began to discuss issues like justice and renewal. However, none of them understood how laws were made or how paperwork worked. They became frustrated with all the forms. Eventually, they left, flying back to their trees.

At first, the animals thought they could fix the systems that humans built. But they quickly realized that systems built on fear, greed, and complexity couldn't simply be fixed by having *wings or paws.*

"Why do they need ten steps to do something good?" grumbled a **lion**, walking out of a **government building** in **Brazil**, shaking his head.

"It's like they trapped themselves in their own system," muttered a **chimpanzee**, poking at a **vending machine** that refused to light up.

Some animals tried to take over **hospitals**, others wandered into **schools**, and one **raccoon** even managed to drive a subway train for three stops before everything went wrong. A **bear** accidentally triggered a fire alarm, and a **giraffe** knocked over a **telecom tower** with its long neck.

It wasn't really funny, but it also wasn't tragic. It was something different... *enlightening*!

Zephyr, soaring high above the chaos, observed everything from a distance. *"We thought we wanted what they had,"* he said quietly to himself. *"But maybe they never had it at all."*

Fractures Among the Feathered

Not all animals agreed on what to do next...

Some, like Zephyr, believed the best approach was to sit back, observe, and gently guide the world towards a brighter future. He truly understood that both humans and animals needed time to heal, rather than strict control.

For him, the path forward wasn't about domination; it was about fostering understanding. Zephyr felt that helping everyone find their balance was far more important than attempting to replace humans.

However, he recognized that not everyone shared this perspective.

A different eagle named **Kato** had a completely different idea. *"They had their chance to rule the earth for too long,"* He said, his sharp eyes glowing with determination. *"Now it's our turn. We are the ones who deserve to lead."*

Kato had a following. He believed that now was the time for the animals to take control. *"Let's take what's ours,"* he said to his supporters.

This led to arguments between the two groups of eagles...

Abibi, trying to keep things calm, warned, *"If we grab power too quickly, it will poison us. We didn't suffer all this time just to become the same as those we hated."*

But Kato's supporters weren't listening. They were tired of being ignored. They wanted cities, tall buildings, and to rule, just like the humans once did.

Soon, different groups began to form—**birds of prey** started claiming territories and formed **"sky councils"** to divide the world. Some apes marched together like armies as if they were preparing for war. Even the peaceful dolphins began debating whether they should establish boundaries in the oceans.

Old instincts that the animals thought they had left behind were coming back.

Jealousy... Power struggles... Arrogance...

The very things they had once hated in humans were now creeping up within them...

Akiiki, known for his wisdom and thoughtfulness, looked around at the rising tension. He shook his head with a heavy heart, feeling a deep sadness. *"Are we really no better than they were? Or are we just the next ones to fall into the same trap?"*

Zephyr's Lament

As the sun set behind the mountains, Zephyr sat on a tall rock, his wings tucked closely against him. His keen gaze surveyed the landscape below, but today, he felt no excitement for flight. The air was unnaturally calm, and the distant sounds of turmoil echoed in, becoming more pronounced with every moment.

He had witnessed the animals taking on human roles, the emergence of new orders, and the rush for power. Initially, the Flip appeared as a chance to reset the world from human arrogance. However, the more Zephyr observed, the more he questioned whether the animals were surrendering to the same traps.

<u>Was this really freedom?</u>

<u>Or</u>

<u>Was it just another form of control?</u>

"I thought the truth would free us," Zephyr whispered to the wind, his voice thick with uncertainty. *"But it feels like we're drowning in it."*

Below him, in the valley, he saw the remnants of human life. People were sleeping in unusual places—burrows and parks, alongside animals they had once owned. The children who had once been pampered were now seeking comfort in the wild. The entire world had changed, but Zephyr wasn't sure if it was for the better.

Despite the confusion, a strange stillness lingered. The humans appeared to awaken. They weren't ruling or suffering but began to see the world differently and understand their place. For the first time, there was no rush, anxiety, or need to control.

Zephyr's wings twitched, as if something inside him was stirring. He had always believed in the need for change, for awakening.

<u>But this?</u>

This wasn't what he had imagined...

This wasn't the world he had hoped for...

<u>He closed his eyes, remembering the Great I Am's original call:</u>
The Flip was not meant to replace humans; it was meant to awaken them.

Zephyr's heart felt heavy as the words echoed. Perhaps the Great I Am always knowing this would happen—humans and animals trapped in their power cycles. Maybe the Flip wasn't about one side winning, but understanding the lost balance.

A familiar voice broke his thoughts. *"Zephyr?"* Abibi's voice was soft but carried across the wind. He turned to see her perched beside him, her feathers glowing in the fading light.

"You're overthinking again," she said, a gentle smile lighting up her beak. *"It's not all about control. Not everything has to be a struggle."*

Zephyr sighed, his gaze still fixed on the horizon. *"I know, Abibi. But I wonder... Are we any better than humans? We fought for freedom, but now, it feels like we're fighting for control."*

Abibi tilted her head, considering his words, *"Maybe we need to stop fighting altogether. Maybe this moment—this world—is a chance to start fresh, to rebuild, not just as rulers but as partners. The hardest part, Zephyr, is not taking control. It's knowing when to let go."*

Zephyr looked at her, his wings slightly unfurled as he took in the weight of her words. It wasn't about leadership or being at the top; it was about learning to live and coexist.

The hardest part was not the fight, but the quiet moments of understanding that followed. As the stars twinkled, Zephyr realized this was the beginning of a new world, governed by awareness, not power.

The Silence That Followed

When all the shouting settled and the chaos faded into the background, a peaceful silence embraced the space. It wasn't just empty; it was rich with meaning, full of the weight of the words spoken, the actions taken, and even those left unspoken. It was a silence that gently invited reflection rather than demanded to be filled.

Across hills and hollowed cities, across rivers that once ran black, a pause blanketed the earth. The rush to replace, rebuild, and reclaim slowed. Animals stopped drawing borders, and humans ceased pretending they knew what they were doing.

<u>**Something softer took root:**</u> *Stillness.*

Not every creature welcomed it. For some, stillness felt like weakness...

However, Zephyr, watching from the edge of a jagged cliff, recognized it for what it truly was: *A seed. Not yet a tree. Not even a sprout. But it's a beginning.*

For the first time, no one was demanding to lead...

No one was rushing to be saved...

It was a time without councils, riots, or speeches, creating a sense of quiet and stillness...

Just one long breath, drawn together—across species, across stories...

The silence wasn't a sign of defeat. It was a choice to listen...

And that, at last, felt new...

Chapter 9
The Final Revelation

For the first time in remembered existence, nothing moved—not out of fear, but out of understanding. The noise of striving had quieted, replaced not with emptiness but with presence. Birds no longer imitated businessmen, and the lions no longer roared orders.

Even the ants, once feverishly busy, paused in their paths. What filled the space was not silence but awareness. It wasn't surrender; it was clarity. The world hadn't given up; it had finally tuned in.

And in that rare, collective exhale, something true finally had room to speak...

In this quiet awakening, something remarkable began to take shape—not through declarations or divine thunder, but through a hush that spoke louder than words. It arrived like sunlight through fog: soft, steady, and undeniable.

The message didn't need to be heard to be understood. The Great I Am's final lesson wasn't taught; it was absorbed—woven into the very stillness that now cradled the world.

Hearts didn't race with revelation; they remembered something they'd long forgotten...

The Great I Am's Ultimate Lesson: The Human Chase

The first part of the lesson was about *humans*. As they stumbled through this new, stripped-down reality, relying on instincts they barely remembered, the reason for their never-ending dissatisfaction became glaringly obvious. It wasn't about having too little; it was about chasing the wrong things.

<u>They had built towering cities, intricate systems, and powerful machines, all in pursuit of... what?</u>

More. Always more. More money, more comfort, more approval, more speed, more noise and only more…

They want more…

They were like hamsters on a wheel, running faster and faster, convinced that happiness was just around the next bend, never realizing that the wheel wasn't actually going anywhere.

Take **Brenda**, the former marketing executive. Before the Flip, her mornings began with checking stock prices and ended with strategizing how to make people desire things they didn't need. Her worth was measured in quarterly reports and market share.

Now, her day starts with the chill of the morning air and the search for clean water. One dawn, huddled by a small fire, she watched a spider meticulously weave its web. No frantic energy, no complaints about deadlines—*just patient, focused creation.*

Brenda felt a small ache in her heart. Her entire life had revolved around crafting intricate, unseen webs of desire in the minds of others, while this spider simply created what it needed to thrive, beautifully and honestly. The spider wasn't pursuing a larger web or seeking more *'likes'* from other spiders; it was simply... *living.*

Brenda came to understand that her unyielding pursuit had left her feeling completely empty, much like a beautifully wrapped gift with nothing inside.

Then there was **Mike**, the social media addict. His world had been a curated feed of other people's highlight reels—a constant comparison game he always lost. He'd chased likes as if they were lifeblood, convinced that external validation would fill the hole inside him.

Now, without his phone, the silence felt profound. He found himself looking people in the eye and truly listening to their genuine voices, rather than just skimming through their thoughtfully crafted captions.

One night, as they sat around a cosy fire sharing a humble meal, someone began sharing a simple story about watching fireflies. It may not have been thrilling or trending, but it was undeniably real.

In that shared moment of quiet wonder, Mike felt a connection that went so much deeper than any online interaction. He noticed the tired lines on the storyteller's face and the genuine smile that radiated warmth, highlighting our shared humanity. It dawned on him that the *'connection'* he'd pursued online was just a flimsy imitation—*like trying to hug a ghost.*

True connection is beautifully messy, imperfect, and unfolds right here, in those quiet, unedited moments that we often treasure the most.

Across the globe, similar scenes unfolded…

A famous musician, accustomed to screaming crowds and flashing lights, found himself captivated by the intricate song of a single bird.

A powerful politician, stripped of his security detail and podium, felt a strange sense of relief as he observed ants working together, a silent, efficient collaboration he'd never comprehended in the halls of power.

A brilliant scientist, whose life revolved around equations and theories, was brought to tears by the simple, perfect geometry of a snowflake.

The lesson was sinking in, not through lectures but through raw experience...

Humans were restless, always chasing because they sought happiness, purpose, and connection in all the wrong places—outside themselves, in things, in status, and in the approval of others. They had built a world designed to keep them running, a perpetual motion machine of dissatisfaction.

And the Great I Am had simply... unplugged it...

The Divine Insight: The Animals' Gift of Peace

The second part of the lesson was the mirror image of the first. As humans grappled with the emptiness of their chase, the animals embodied the very thing they craved: harmony.

Perched on their cliff, Zephyr, Abibi, and Akiiki felt this truth in their bones. They didn't need to be taught harmony; they lived it. They were woven into the fabric of the world, not separate from it.

Akiiki, watching a hawk circle effortlessly below, chirped, *"See? The hawk isn't worried about whether it's the best hawk or if other hawks have more shiny things. It just flies. It hunts. It is. There's no 'should be' or 'could be,' just 'is.'"*

He witnessed the hawk dive, swift and true, for its prey—*a life-and-death struggle that was simply part of the natural order, not a source of existential dread or comparison.*

Abibi nodded, her golden eyes thoughtful.

"We tried to take over, didn't we? We thought we could do it better, run their systems. But their systems were built on the very things that made them unhappy – competition, accumulation, and control. We

almost got caught in the same trap.”

She recalled chaotic attempts to mimic human power structures and the arguments among animals about leadership. It now felt silly and sad. They realized that power wasn't about ruling others; it was about fully being present and capable in your own skin, feathers, or scales.

Zephyr, the oldest and wisest, spoke softly.

"The Great I Am didn't flip the world to give us power. The Great I Am flipped the world to show humans what they had lost, and to remind us of what we already have."

He looked at his wings, at the sky, at the world spread out below.

"We offer the harmony they seek. We embody the balance they have overlooked."

He thought of **Elara**, an old elk he knew, whose life was a quiet rhythm of grazing, migrating, and caring for her herd. She didn't worry about the future beyond the changing seasons. She didn't compare her antlers to those of another elk.

Her life had a simple, profound dignity that came from being exactly what she was, where she was meant to be.

He thought of **Finn**, a playful dolphin, whose days were filled with the simple joy of swimming and finding food. Finn wasn't striving for anything more than a full belly and a good slide down a muddy bank. His happiness was immediate and uncomplicated.

Animals lived in the present…

They took only what they needed…

They were connected to their environment, to the cycles of life and death, growth and decay. They did not create problems where none existed. They did not fight over imaginary lines or invisible numbers. Their lives possessed a fundamental peace that humans seemed incapable of finding within their own complex world.

This realization resonated deeply with the animals…

They had been so caught up in humans' mistakes and frustrations that they hadn't truly embraced the incredible wisdom of their existence. They didn't have to become human to find fulfilment; they already possessed it in their own unique way.

Harmony wasn't just something to seek or create; it was simply something to embody…

The Big Question: Do We Still Want to Be Human?

As the stillness deepened and the Great I Am's lesson settled fully into the hearts and minds of animals everywhere, a significant question arose. It wasn't a voice but a collective thought, a shared contemplation that rippled through the animal kingdom:

<u>Do we still want to be human?</u>

This wasn't just a simple yes or no; it was a pretty complex situation, filled with everything they had experienced and felt. The initial urge to take over and show humans the ropes was starting to fade.

They had witnessed the weight of the human world, the self-inflicted struggles, and the endless, empty pursuit of more.

Yet, in those quiet moments of the Flip, they glimpsed the potential for human connection and simple joy, even if it felt buried beneath layers of their own *creation.*

Some animals, those who had briefly savoured the taste of human-like power or comfort, hesitated…

Leo, the proud lion who had briefly lorded over an empty zoo, felt a pang of regret for the easy meals and the admiring stares. He missed the feeling of effortless dominance, even if it was over empty cages.

Penny, the pampered poodle who had enjoyed soft beds and endless treats, whined softly, missing the warmth of a human lap and the infinite supply of kibble.

For them, the human world, despite its flaws, provided a comfort they hadn't found in the wild...

Most animals, sensing the deep peace of nature and the satisfaction of balance, felt a different answer rise within them. They saw the struggling humans trying to light a fire or find food, feeling pity and relief that this wasn't their natural state.

A great whale, deep in the ocean, sent a thought that resonated with ancient wisdom: *We swim in the vastness, we sing our songs, we are connected to the pulse of the sea. Why would we trade this for tiny boxes and endless noise? Their world is loud and shallow. Ours is deep and quiet.*

A wolf, running free through the forest, felt the wind in its fur and the earth beneath its paws: *We hunt, we run, we live with our pack. We are free. Their world felt like a cage, even for them. They were trapped by things, by worries, by each other.*

A bird, soaring high above the mountains, felt the sheer joy of flight: *We dance on the wind, we see the world from above, we sing with the dawn. Their world kept them grounded, heavy with things they didn't need. Why would we choose to be heavy?*

Most animals realised they didn't want to be human, rejecting endless striving and dissatisfaction, feeling no burden in chasing

<u>**inconsequential things because they already had what mattered:**</u> *presence, connection to the earth, and the simple peace of being.*

On the cliff, Zephyr, Abibi, and Akiiki experienced a powerful realization. A wave of *acceptance and contentment* washed over the animal kingdom. The desire to replace humans faded, replaced by quiet confidence in their own way of life.

"No," Abibi whispered, knowing it was true.

"We don't." Her ambition to control vanished, replaced by the desire to fly, hunt, and be an eagle.

Akiiki responded, *"Nope! Being a bird is far cooler than a Screamy Steve! Or a lonely Mike with no likes! They just can't imagine sacrificing the amazing freedom of the sky for a glowing rectangle or a pile of paper money."*

Zephyr looked up at the sky, feeling a deep sense of peace. The lesson from the Great I Am was meant for both humans and animals. They were shown the human path but opted to forge their own. This test highlighted not only humanity's shortcomings but also the animal world's inborn perfection.

The Unseen Shift and The Gathering Storm

As this understanding took root in the animal kingdom, a subtle change emerged. The dark shadow that had been sustained by human negativity seemed to retreat, diminishing slightly. It thrived on discontent and the pursuit of misguided desires. As people began to find true peace and animals regained their natural harmony, the shadow diminished, similar to a parasite without its host.

But it wasn't gone—*not entirely.* It remained at the edges of the world, a dark, patient presence waiting. It thrived on the potential for negativity, on the chance that humans could forget and animals could fail.

The Great I Am's presence reemerged, not through words but as a new sensation. It was a feeling of transition.

The pause was coming to an end...

Phase One, humanity's trial, was ending. The lessons were imparted, and the animals had chosen.

And Phase Two was coming...

This next phase wasn't about flipping the world again, with animals taking over or humans immediately returning to their old ways. It was about the *interaction* between the two worlds, changed as they now were. The experiment wasn't over; it was just evolving.

The animals had learned their lesson about the value of their existence and the emptiness of the human chase. They were grounded, centered, and filled with the quiet confidence of their natural state. The humans had begun to remember, stumbling and confused, what it meant to simply be, to connect, and to rely on the earth and each other. They were raw, vulnerable, and stripped of their defenses.

Now, they would come together, transformed by their journeys. The Great I Am was gently drawing the two worlds closer, not as *ruler and ruled*, but as *fellow beings* sharing the same beautiful planet, both having learned important, though sometimes difficult, lessons.

Imagine the moment when humbled and bare humans meet the animals, filled with the quiet confidence of their own natural wisdom. What a fascinating encounter that would be!

<u>Would humans, after experiencing a different life, be open to learning from the creatures they once dismissed?</u>

<u>**Would the animals, seeing both darkness and light in the human heart, guide them, or would old resentments surface?**</u>

The air on the plateau began to hum with a refreshing energy, one that was different from the chaotic vibe of the Flip. This new feeling was filled with anticipation, uncertainty, and a delightful charge of possibility. It brings to mind that peaceful moment just before a storm, where everything seems to come together, *not in anger, but with a thrilling and unpredictable energy.*

Zephyr, Abibi, and Akiiki felt it deeply. Their mission wasn't finished yet; it was just stepping into its most crucial phase. They had started as messengers, then moved on to observers, and finally became participants in a global awakening. *Now, they were on the brink of transforming into...*

Something new...

<u>**Perhaps guides?**</u>

<u>**Maybe mediators?**</u>

<u>**Witnesses to humanity's final choice?**</u>

Zephyr gazed at Abibi, his wise eyes sparkling with a blend of hope and a touch of worry. *"They are waking up,"* he said softly, almost like a secret.

"But the path ahead... It's still a mystery. Will they remember? Will they embrace the gentle harmony instead of the noisy chase?"

Abibi met his gaze, her golden eyes reflecting the setting sun. *"We must be ready,"* she replied, her voice firm. *"We must be ready to... guide, teach, connect, and show them the harmony, not just tell them about it."*

Akiiki, no longer just the curious youngster, felt a surge of quiet determination, mixed with a flutter of fear. *"We showed them what they lost,"* he chirped. *"Now... we show them what they can find. But what if they don't want to find it?"*

As the last rays of sunshine gently dipped below the horizon, casting warm shadows across the beautifully transformed world, the Great I Am's final, unspoken message of this phase embraced them: *The lesson has been revealed. The choice has been made (by the animals)... Now, the meeting begins... And the human choice...*

And then, the stillness on the plateau broke; not with a sound, but with a feeling of acceleration, of time beginning to move forward again.

The pause was over...

Below, the world stirred with a sense of purpose. Humans, feeling raw and vulnerable, started to move, but this time not with the frantic energy of before; instead, they took hesitant steps, looking around and looking up. Animals, now grounded in their newfound certainty, gazed out at the horizon, watching where they knew the humans were gathering.

Two worlds, beautifully transformed, were on the brink of coming together. Not through conflict, but through a meaningful encounter. An encounter that would encourage humans to gaze into the eyes of the creatures they had overlooked and rediscover the peace they had *forgotten*. This encounter would challenge the animals' patience and their generous spirit to share their *timeless wisdom*.

<u>What would happen when the creatures of harmony met the beings who were beginning to remember what harmony felt like?</u>

Would the lessons stick?

Will the change last?

Or will the old ways creep back in, stronger, feeding on this new uncertainty?

The answer lay not in the past or even entirely in the present but in the uncertain, thrilling, and potentially heartbreaking moments that were about to unfold.

The stage was set, the characters changed, and the final act was about to begin...

As Zephyr, Abibi, and Akiiki gazed at the first timid movements of the converging worlds below, a chilling realization washed over them: *The shadow was getting stronger again, drawn by the amazing and delicate potential of this encounter.*

Its shape, once a bit unclear, now looked more defined around the edges, hinting at a presence that flourished on the very excitement of this unpredictable future.

No one—neither human nor animal, not even the wise old eagles—knew how it would end or what role the growing darkness would play.

The eagle's last flight neared, but its destination and the world's fate hung in the balance...

The time has come for a new beginning, the one set by The Great I Am...

Chapter 10
The Eagle's Last Flight

So, listen closely, because this is where everything comes to a head. That wild, wacky experiment, the one where the animals essentially took over and humans experienced life on the wild side.

Yeah, that whole thing is officially over. The cosmic timer has hit zero, the big clock in the sky just gave its final ding, and everyone's wondering the same thing.

<u>Did any of it truly stick after all this madness, all this flipping and flopping?</u>

It's really worth asking! After all that wild role reversal, the surprising lessons, and the complete, delightful chaos... did we humans, the ones who believed we had everything in order... **<u>finally, finally wake up?</u>**

<u>Have we truly opened our eyes to see the mess we've created— the beautiful, vibrant world we've been rushing through, and the peaceful, simple life we've somehow lost touch with?</u>

Or

<u>Is this just another weird dream you shake off, blink a few times, and then go back to chasing your tail, glued to your phone, stressing about deadlines, and forgetting to live?</u>

High above the world, Zephyr, Abibi, and Akiiki—our eagle pals, the messengers who have seen it all—look down. They're ready to drop their final big message on humanity. And let me tell you, it's not just fluffy clouds and happy thoughts.

<u>It's a real cocktail:</u> *A heavy dose of wisdom, a splash of "are you* *kidding me with this?" humor, and a whole lot of "okay, we're out, good luck with all that." They've been through the wringer too, watching humanity stumble, fall, and occasionally, surprisingly, rise… it's been a show. And they're prepared for their final bow.*

The World: Fresh Out the Dryer

The world feels different now…

It's not a Hollywood blockbuster with explosions and quick rebuilds. It's elusive, like waking from a long, confusing dream; the room looks the same but feels different.

<u>The crazy rush?</u>

<u>The constant hustle and bustle?</u>

It's dialed down… Way down…

People walk, not sprint like their hair's on fire. They look up at the sky, clouds, and trees instead of staring at small screens.

<u>You see people talking face-to-face—no emojis, no texts, just real words. Wild, right?</u>

<u>The cities themselves?</u>

Man, they've gotten a serious makeover…

They're not just cold, gray concrete jungles anymore. They're, like, *actual* jungles, in some spots. Green stuff is *everywhere*. Vines are climbing up skyscrapers, turning them into these crazy vertical gardens. Flowers are busting through cracks in the sidewalks, like nature's just decided, *"Nope, this is our turf now."*

<u>And the air?</u>

Oh man, the air smells cleaner…

It feels as if someone finally opened all the windows on the entire planet and let fresh air circulate. It's refreshing, like after a summer rain, not that musty exhaust smell we used to inhale without a second thought.

And the people?

They're… softer, somehow…

There is less stress and less on edge. You notice more sincere smiles, more people relaxing, and taking a moment to breathe. It's as if they are rediscovering how to simply exist rather than constantly needing to accomplish something. This is a subtle revolution. They're observing their surroundings, assisting one another, and creating small community gardens where skyscrapers once loomed large.

It may be chaotic, but it is authentic!

Signs of Hope

Akiiki, with her super-sharp eagle eyes, spots something that makes her heart flutter with happiness.

In what used to be a beautifully kept, fenced-off park, a joyful group of kids is playing—really playing!

They're not glued to tablets or staring at their phones; instead, they're running, laughing, climbing trees, and inventing their own games.

She turns to **Zephyr**, a rare, gentle smile on her beak. *"They're starting to remember,"* she chirps, and there's this fragile, powerful hope in her voice.

Zephyr nods slowly, his ancient eyes scanning the horizon. *"The old ways are fading,"* he observes, his voice a low rumble like distant thunder.

"But what they replace them with... that's the real trick. That's entirely up to them now."

The shadow, a creepy presence drawn to chaos, seemed to retreat, less sure of this unpredictable reality. For the first time, the choice felt truly *humane.*

<u>The animals, briefly acting as *"humans,"* had given mankind a gift:</u>

A mirror...

What they saw in that mirror was the key...

The Eagle's Last Stand

The time for talk is almost over...

The eagles gather everyone for one last, epic pow-wow...

They chose this amazing spot on a high cliff that offers a breathtaking view of a sprawling city, where the concrete jungle beautifully meets the wild, untamed wilderness.

It's just perfect!

It's a wonderful reminder that humans and nature are meant to work together harmoniously. In this space, the wind gracefully carries the gentle hum of human life alongside the soft whispers of the trees.

They're not talking to everyone...

Only those who truly showed they were engaged, the ones who weren't merely counting down the minutes until they could return to their lattes and stock portfolios.

There's **Jan**, the artist, whose hands are stained with the vibrant colors of a world being reborn. Her art isn't just pretty pictures anymore; it's alive. It's about connection and how everything fits together. Her canvases literally bloom with life.

Then there's **Seth**, the musician, whose guitar isn't just creating catchy tunes now. His melodies are deep and soulful, carrying the very pulse of the earth. His music makes you want to hug a tree, dance barefoot in the grass, and truly feel the world around you.

And...

Mimilo, the dancer, used to move with sharp, controlled, almost robotic movements. Now, she dances with the untamed grace of the wind, her body flowing like a river, telling the story of the earth's ancient rhythms and its endless cycles of growth and renewal. She's a living, breathing testament to newfound freedom.

Finally, there's **Gege**, our exceptional community leader! He's not just leading committees anymore; he's actively engaging with communities on the ground. He's bringing people together to share and support each other. With his efforts, he's fostering a beautiful sense of belonging, making everyone feel that they're all in this together. His voice, which used to be merely a drone in a boardroom, now resonates with a powerful rumble of unity and understanding.

These four examples show us just how amazing things can be...

They represent hope for all of us!

Words of Wisdom

Zephyr steps forward, perched on a weathered outcrop, his ancient eyes locking with theirs. His booming voice carries surprising gentleness. *"We didn't come here to judge you,"* he begins, giving them that classic eagle stare that could make a rock feel guilty.

"We came to give you a wake-up call. Let's be honest," he adds, a hint of dry amusement, *"you've been hitting the snooze button for a*

very long time."

A few nervous chuckles ripple through the small crowd; he pauses, allowing those words to settle in, then continues, his gaze lovingly sweeping over the revitalized land.

"You are a species of magnificent contradictions. You're capable of breathtaking beauty, of soaring creativity, of acts of selfless courage that defy logic. You reach for the stars, you unlock the secrets of the universe, you create art that moves souls."

He sighs, like wind through ancient canyons, *"and yet, you possess a remarkable talent for self-destruction. You build incredible cities, towering testaments to ingenuity, then forget how to live in them, breathe in them, or truly belong to them. You invent amazing technologies, tools that could connect you to the universe, yet use them to disconnect from each other, the earth, and your own souls."*

Abibi, bursting with youthful enthusiasm, can't contain herself. She charges ahead, her voice electrified with passion. *"You were so focused on chasing progress that you completely lost sight of purpose!"* she declares, spreading her wings wide.

"You were consumed by possessions, gadgets, and trends—status symbols in relentless accumulation! Yet, you overlooked experiences that truly enrich life! You sought happiness in a mythical 'someday' instead of embracing the present's breathtaking beauty! It resembled a golden retriever spinning in circles, frantically chasing its tail—a tiresome pursuit for something unattainable. It was… exhausting to witness!"

Akiiki, her voice clear as a mountain spring, delivers the crucial part of their message. *"The true measure of a life well-lived isn't about how much you own, power you wield, or followers you have on ridiculous platforms. That's just noise."* She pauses, letting her words hang.

"It's about remembering your inner capacity for love, compassion, humility, and connection. It's about living in harmony and unity, not just with each other, though that's a fantastic start, but with everything on this fragile planet: trees, rivers, mountains, insects, birds, and the air you breathe. You are not separate from this world but an integral part of it. Your fate is linked to its fate."

She pauses, her luminous eyes scanning the humans before her, expressing a mix of hope, concern, and weary resignation. *"The choice, as always, is yours. You can retreat to your old ways, your insatiable hunger for more, your stubborn insistence on control, your delusion of conquering a world infinitely more powerful and ancient than you. You can try to put the genie back in the bottle, but you can't un-see what you've seen, right?"*

She smiles knowingly. *"Or,"* she says softly, *"you can choose a different path. A path of humility, respect, interconnectedness, balance, simplicity, and genuine caring. A path where the wisdom of the animals is not just a quaint idea, but a guiding principle. The world."*

She looks over the landscape and concludes, *"It is holding its breath, waiting to see what you will do next. Don't… for the love of all that is holy… screw it up."*

The Grand Finale

With that final, powerful declaration, the eagles soar into the sky…

It's more than just wings flapping; it's a rising…

They rise into the vast, boundless sky, their mighty wings catching the last rays of the setting sun. Their impressive shadows contrast brightly with the blazing twilight sky, crafting a stunning and conclusive scene.

They leave behind a world that has changed forever, a world that has been granted an excellent second chance, and a world that finds itself at an exciting crossroads, ready to embrace a brand-new future.

The formal experiment has come to an end... It's complete!

After fulfilling their roles, the animals found their patience tested and their horizons expanded. Now, they joyfully return to their respective habitats, carrying with them the unforgettable memories of this extraordinary adventure that has transformed them.

You can bet they'll have some epic stories to share around the watering hole, or the communal nest, or whatever the animal equivalent of a campfire tale might be!

Remember that time humans were squirrels?

Man, those guys were terrible at burying nuts!

The humans are on a journey now, working through the outcome, sifting through the ruins of their old ways, and embarking on the exciting yet challenging and honestly quite scary process of building a new one.

The lessons of the Great Flip, the raw, undeniable wisdom imparted by the eagles, and the stark reality of their interconnectedness with the natural world—*these elements won't be easily forgotten.*

These moments have become deeply etched in humanity's shared memories, reminding us of that incredible day when the animals spoke, the world paused in awe, and everything transformed. Though the shadow remains, weakened but not entirely gone, it quietly lingers at the edges, constantly reminding us of the darkness that could return if we ever lose our way.

So, the eagles' last flight isn't merely a neat ending with all the loose ends tied up in a pretty bow. Instead, it's more ambiguous, deeper, and incredibly real.

It's a...

A big pause...

A pregnant silence surrounds us, enriched by the gentle hum of a reawakened planet and the soft whispers of human thought...

It's a moment filled with uncertainty, yes, but it's also overflowing with possibility and hope...

The old world, obsessed with being number one and blind to the bigger picture, is gone. A new world, rooted in understanding and respect, is emerging. The future is a blank canvas, with humans as artists, equipped with the wisdom of the animal kingdom.

The world has been given a second act, a chance to rewrite its own story, to step onto a stage where peace and harmony take center stage rather than merely serving as background noise.

<u>But what happens next?</u>

<u>What choices will humanity make when the eagles are truly gone, when the silence of their absence settles?</u>

I wonder if they will truly embrace the valuable lessons of humility, compassion, and interconnectedness!

<u>Will they create a fresh journey, one that allows them to thrive in harmony with nature and one another?</u>

Or

Will the temptation of the old ways—the captivating call of greed, power, and control—be too hard to resist?

That, my friends, is entirely up to us...

And honestly?

It's such a delightful mix of fear and excitement!

While this episode may have concluded, the most incredible adventure—the heartfelt journey into humanity's future—this is just a beginning!

After all this time...

Earth is finally welcoming a sense of calm and hopeful peace...

The eagles are gone, but their message echoes in the hearts of those who listened:

The future is not written...

It is waiting to be written by you...

Epilogue: *Lessons for the Future*

And just like that, the cosmic clock hit zero...

The grand experiment?

It's over now...

The animals, our unexpected teachers, packed up and moved on, leaving us, the so-called smartest species, standing there with a simple question echoing in the silence.

Did we actually learn anything?

<u>**Did we finally wake up to the vibrant, aching beauty of the world we'd been stomping over for so long?**</u>

<u>**Or was it just a blip—a short-lived pause before we went back to chasing deadlines and dollar signs?**</u>

<u>The eagles were the last to fly. They didn't roar or demand tribute or power. With a gentle sweep of their wings, they gifted us a message:</u> *It wasn't loud, but it was beautifully clear…*

This wasn't about control…

It was about balance…

*It was all about **Unity**…*

And…

Unity brings peace, harmony, and cooperation, fostering understanding, respect, and empathy among people…

They weren't here to dominate. They were here to remind us of something deep, something ancient, something we'd lost touch with. And as they disappeared into the clouds, it seemed as though the entire world held its breath.

After they were gone, things got… *Interesting!*

Some people got it…

You could see it in their eyes…

Farmers began growing food with their hands again, not just relying on machines. People in cities walked more, drove less, and stopped actually to look at the sky. The air smelled cleaner. Oceans sparkled. Rivers, long choked and tired, began to dance again.

It felt like Earth itself was letting out a long, overdue sigh…

Finally, someone was listening…

But not everyone did…

Let's be real…

Old habits are stubborn things…

That never-ending itch for more—the next big thing, the next promotion, the next distraction—it's hardwired into so many of us. Some have slipped back into the same grind.

Same greed, same illusion that we can somehow outrun emptiness by filling it with things. That if we just hustle a little harder, we'll finally be happy. Spoiler alert: we never are.

And yet…

Something had changed…

<u>A quiet shift occurred in people's thinking. They realized something important—perhaps the most important thing of all:</u> *Real knowledge is not about how much you know, but about how deeply you feel. Peace does not come from possessing everything; it comes from understanding when you have enough.*

Real power isn't control, it's responsibility!

<u>And connection?</u>

It doesn't glow from a screen…

It arises from making eye contact, sharing moments of comfortable silence together, and being *truly* present with one another.

So…

<u>Where does that leave us?</u>

The animals are gone...

Their voices are quiet now...

<u>But the message?</u>

It's still here...

Still humming underneath everything...

Waiting...

Note it in your diary: *The future isn't set in stone; it's a blank page, and we're the ones holding the pen.*

It's scary, sure, but also incredibly exciting...

<u>Will we rise to the moment?</u>

<u>Or fall back into the comfort of our chaos?</u>

The truth is, maybe the animals had it figured out all along...

They don't overthink...

They don't hoard or destroy...

They eat when they're hungry...

Sleep when they're tired...

And...

Play when they feel joy...

They live in rhythm with the world, not against it...

And maybe, just maybe, that's the real secret we've been missing...

This wasn't the end, not even a close chapter yet...

It was a wake-up call…

A spark…

A second chance…

Now it's sour turn to choose better and to live brighter…

To remember what it means to be alive…

The canvas is beautifully wide open, inviting us to let our imagination flow. The colors are right at our fingertips, ready for us to create something amazing together!

Let's paint something beautiful…